From (

Raised on a daily dose of _____
experimentation, Ramgopal 'RamG' Vallath _____
early: one should never take oneself too seriously, and no problem is unsolvable.

Soon, he was whizzing through life, having got an all-India 129th rank in the Indian Institute of Technology Joint Entrance Examination (IIT-JEE). The fact that he did an extended five-year B.Tech. from IIT Madras did not have anything to do with his love for the subject. Having figured out that electronics was not his cup of tea, he jumped into the management rat race to do an MBA from the Xavier Labour Relations Institute in Jamshedpur.

He went on to build a successful corporate career, becoming a COO in Airtel at thirty-five, one of the youngest circle heads in India's telecom industry. Not satisfied with the level of challenge in life, he also got diagnosed with a rare autoimmune disorder which crippled him.

Never one to give up, he kept up a positive outlook. Over the next ten years, even as he grappled with his deteriorating health, he continued to hold down tough and complex jobs, first as a director at Dell and then at HP. In his quest for improved fitness, he lost 12 kg and taught himself how to swim by watching YouTube videos.

He now maintains a busy travel schedule as a motivational speaker and has addressed thousands of children as well as corporate employees, making them laugh out loud as he shared life-changing lessons. He presently consults for the Azim Premji Foundation and works at a Bangalore-based start-up called Zentron Labs in the field of machine vision. It helps companies improve the quality of their production by enabling 100 per cent quality inspection at high speeds using computer vision and software.

He is also the author of a wacky and humorous science fantasy novel called *Oops the Mighty Gurgle*.

Tweet while you read @ramgvallath. Use #Ouch2oops.

From Ouch to Oops

RamG Vallath

COLLINS
BUSINESS

First published in India in 2014 by Collins Business
An imprint of HarperCollins *Publishers*

Copyright © Ramgopal Vallath 2014

P-ISBN: 978-93-5136-817-5
E-ISBN: 978-93-5136-818-2

2 4 6 8 10 9 7 5 3

Ramgopal Vallath asserts the moral right to be
identified as the author of this work.

HarperCollins *Publishers*

A-75, Sector 57, Noida, Uttar Pradesh 201301, India
1 London Bridge Street, London SE1 9GF, United Kingdom
Hazelton Lanes, 55 Avenue Road, Suite 2900, Toronto, Ontario M5R 3L2
and 1995 Markham Road, Scarborough, Ontario M1B 5M8, Canada
25 Ryde Road, Pymble, Sydney, NSW 2073, Australia
195 Broadway, New York, NY 10007, USA

Typeset in 12/15 Adobe Garamond Pro at
SÜRYA, New Delhi

Printed and bound at
Thomson Press (India) Ltd.

This book is dedicated to all the protons in the universe who continue to remain positive in spite of the negativity whizzing around them

Contents

Ouch

The meeting was scheduled for 8 a.m. I was up at 5 a.m. Not because I was a health freak and had to stand on my head in a complex yoga pose or sweat it out in the gym for an hour. I just had to take a bath, have my breakfast and, most important, do up the six buttons of the shirt I would wear—three tasks that any healthy person would have completed in thirty minutes or less.

But I needed three hours because of my condition: CIDP, short for Chronic Inflammatory Demyelinating Polyneuropathy, a rare autoimmune disorder which weakened my arms and legs.

This was in 2009 and I was Director, Volume Operations, for HP India. It was my first meeting in Singapore with the Asia Pacific leadership team, and I did not want to run the risk of appearing too casual by putting on a T-shirt. So there was no way of avoiding the six buttons.

I had planned it all out meticulously. I would order the breakfast at 5.15 a.m., finish my shower before room service arrived, then put on my clothes and finish the breakfast—all by 7.30 a.m., so that I could be in office well in time for the meeting.

But even before I could get to the buttons, my calculations started to go completely awry. I had to pull a small steel lever to start the flow of water from the shower head, and my fingers just did not have the strength for that. I first tried to pull the lever with my left hand, then with my right, and then with both. By this time, I had broken into a sweat but the shower did not start.

The mild jetlag had acutely worsened my condition, and my hands and fingers were almost useless and trembling uncontrollably. I decided to abandon the bath. I quickly soaked a towel and started to wipe myself clean as best as I could. Holding the heavy water-soaked towel and moving it up and down my body was quite a challenge. But I managed to complete the sponge bath just in time to open the door, wrapped in a towel, for room service.

And then it was time for the most excruciatingly difficult task. I had to put on a shirt. I slipped it on and closed my eyes in a silent prayer to Lord Ganesh, the remover of obstacles. I knew that I needed all the help that I could get. My hands trembling uncontrollably, I reached for the top button with my right hand while holding the buttonhole with my left. With every fibre of my being focused on the act of positioning the button exactly next to the buttonhole, I tried again and again to push it through, but in vain.

Over the next half hour, I must have attempted this at least ten times. But each time, the right thumb failed to muster sufficient strength to push the button through. It kept slipping out of my weak fingers.

After every minute, I would have to drop my hands

because my biceps did not have enough strength to hold them up. After a fruitless half an hour, I decided to try doing up the buttons while lying in bed so that I did not have to hold my hands up. It was also easier to position the button exactly next to the buttonhole this way. Finally, after another half hour of sweating, trembling and struggling, I managed to do the top button.

It took me ninety minutes to finish buttoning up the entire shirt. By the time I was ready, I knew that there was no time to have breakfast. At 7.30 a.m., I rushed to the office and managed to reach the conference venue just in time.

But the twenty minutes I spent in the car was all that I needed to recover mentally. I was ready to be the life and soul of the meeting. I had bounced back. I always do. That is why I am the most positive person I have ever met.

1. Problem? Bring It On!

I appreciate that springing the above episode on you without any background was a bit like putting the cart before the horse. So let me step back a bit and present to you the horse. I mean, let me walk you through some events in my life which taught me important lessons and helped shape me. This will also shed some light on the context of what I just described.

To build the horse from scratch, I have to go all the way back and introduce you to my parents. They were the epitome of an average Indian middle class family of the 1970s. My father was an engineer in the Kerala State Electricity Board and my mother was a homemaker (referred to as a housewife in those days of political incorrectness). I had an elder brother, Balagopal Vallath, who was called BalG by everyone. I was born two years after him in 1968. I was called RamG, short for Ramgopal.

After embracing a socialist model, the country had experienced slow economic growth. It was also disconnected from the global economy. Our closest ally was the Soviet Union. The West was, for us, a demon symbolizing greed and colonization.

My parents, like most people of their generation, believed in socialism. They were also extraordinarily idealistic. In a country where caste lines were clear and rigid, they inculcated in us the belief that all human beings are born equal. In a country which has substantial representation of at least five religions and which had witnessed religious strife that caused the deaths of hundreds of thousands of people in just a few decades, they inculcated in us the belief that there is only one god and that all religions are true. In a country where the chasms between classes are unbridgeable, they taught us the concept of respecting every human being and treating everyone as an equal.

My father had strong views about how we should be educated. He insisted on enrolling us in government schools—vernacular ones at that, where every subject was taught in Malayalam, my mother tongue. This was seen as an act of utter stupidity by his peers and relatives. They felt it was the equivalent of flushing us down the drain. Good English-medium education was seen as the only way for the middle class to break barriers and make a quantum leap into the upper or at least the upper-middle class and a government school was not perceived to be capable of delivering the kind of education required for this. Most middle class parents enrolled their kids in privately run or convent schools—the ones run by various parish churches. Consequently, I studied in the type of schools which were abandoned by the upper class and the middle class of society.

Kerala, my home state, was an outlier in many socio-economic parameters compared to the other states of India. In 1956, it had stunned the world by electing the first democratically elected communist government in the world. It had a strong activist middle class and very active trade unions which pushed for better working conditions for the masses. Indices such as the number of doctors per thousand population or number of hospitals per thousand population were comparable to those in developed countries in the West. The literacy rate in Kerala even in those days was nearing 90 per cent while the rest of the country languished at around 50 per cent. Education was given the highest priority, and parents would do anything to ensure that their children were sent to school.

I was one of the privileged few in my school whose fathers were engineers (even though my father's salary in those days was about Rs 2,000 a month). My classmates were mostly from underprivileged backgrounds and many of them had to walk several kilometres through difficult hilly terrain to reach school, often carrying two packets of rice, one for breakfast and one for lunch. There was no school uniform to speak of, except for a white shirt and white mundu, a rectangular piece of cloth which is wrapped around the waist. Nobody ever wore shoes. There were a few students who wore flip-flops, but most could not afford this luxury and were used to walking barefoot. It was not surprising that academically they were far below average, and thanks to the support I had from my parents, my scores were miles ahead of those of my classmates.

One of the pitfalls of using a strong sense of nationalism to drive home the values enshrined in the nation's Constitution is that it makes one believe that one's country is morally superior to others. This was what happened to me. I became a reverse snob. In my mind, much like with many others of my generation, English-medium schooling, urbanization, the private sector, profit making, Western culture, the United States of America, and so on, became things to be looked down upon. Of course, in my case, in addition, I also believed that the Malayali from Kerala was the true proponent of the true religion, communism, and hence superior to all other Indians, who were in turn superior to everyone else (except the Russians). So the pecking order, according to me, was Lenin, Marx, Malayalis, Russians, other Indians and then the rest of the world. Right at the bottom, jostling with the devil, were Americans and the British.

Fortunately for me, this deep dislike for the English-speaking population of the world did not extend to English books. I was a voracious reader and started reading English books when I was about eleven. I was motivated to read the works of P.G. Wodehouse and the stories of Sherlock Holmes in their original form as my father had already introduced me to them in Malayalam. My parents supported our reading habit by enrolling us in public libraries and encouraging us to borrow English books.

A turning point in my life came about when, over some conversation, my father spoke to me about Mark Antony's speech in Shakespeare's *Julius Caesar*. I was so affected by its power that I read the whole play to understand the context. It was bloody difficult, and I must have understood only about 30 per cent of the content. But I took this as a challenge, and by the time I was in Class 10, I had read half a dozen of Shakespeare's plays—all original unabridged versions—and could mutter 'Hark! Methinks thou art a moron' in my sleep. Consequently, my grasp of the English language and its literature was better than that of our teacher, who used to teach us the subject in Malayalam.

One of the clear positive sides of studying in a school where the standards were low was that I had to focus on becoming a good student on an absolute scale, having no clue whatsoever how good or bad I was relative to academically sound kids across the country. In my Class 10 board exams, the pass percentage in my school was an abysmal 20 per cent.

In Class 11 and 12, when I moved to a pre-degree course in a government college (the equivalent of the junior and senior years of high school), the standard improved substantially, but it was still lower than that of the top institutes in the country. Those two years were pure, unadulterated fun. I realized just how much of a nerd I was. This amazing self-realization happened when I started a correspondence coaching programme for the IIT JEE exams.

For those who are not familiar with IIT JEE, or IIT for that matter, let me give a brief explanation. The IITs or the Indian Institutes of Technology—five in my time, sixteen today—were the ultimate destination for undergraduate learning of technology in India. Each year, about 2,00,000 hopeful students would vie for a total of 2,000 seats in these five institutes. Admission was solely based on the Joint Entrance Exam, the IIT JEE, arguably the toughest exam in the universe. It was so tough that a huge number of kids (about a million) who wanted to do their graduation in technology did not even take it and settled for other engineering colleges, knowing full well that they didn't stand a chance of getting through.

I had a huge and unfair advantage. I had no clue about these daunting statistics at that time. I also had no clue about where I stood, since there weren't too many academically strong students of that league around me to compare myself with. Consequently, unfettered by any feeling of inferiority, I dived into the preparation with complete glee.

The other advantage I had, which was almost as important as the earlier one, was that I loved the subjects of study: math and science. Again, I must thank my government school education and my parents for this love of science and my inquisitive nature. The schools I studied in hardly ever loaded me with homework and I had ample time to pursue my scientific curiosities by reading hundreds of science books written in Malayalam and published by an extraordinarily progressive organization called the Kerala Shastra Sahitya Parishad, which worked towards enhancing the standards of education in the state. I also had plenty of opportunities to conduct innumerable experiments on my own using the chemicals, test tubes and other scientific paraphernalia my parents had bought for me at a very young age. (My secret desire was to discover a new element and I spent many hours on this quest, burning various chemicals or mixing them together in our kitchen.)

During the days of my preparation for the IIT entrance exam, I would each month receive a packet from Brilliant Tutorials, a correspondence coaching institute. These had sets of workbooks with problems that were so tough that they would make one's hair curl. But as for me, I attacked them happily. I was a nerd and was proud to be one. There were problems that would knock the living daylights out of me—quite literally, since I would lie awake at night, trying out various permutations and combinations to crack them. But I would never leave a problem unsolved. There were occasions when I spent several days solving a single problem. My distraught mother would think I was heartbroken over some girl and contemplating suicide, when, in actuality, I would be breaking my head over what on earth the value of X was.

But I knew that if I spent enough time on a problem and looked at it from all angles, I would be able to solve it. I used to be so immersed in my preparations that I would often forget to eat or socialize. I was like an athlete who was 'in the zone'. Just in case you think I was a hopeless nerd with no other interests, let me correct you. My friends (a gang of ten boys) and I had tonnes of fun in college. I must have attended about forty hours of class in those two years. The rest of the time was spent in the college canteen or wandering around campus, gawking at girls. (Middle class values in those days frowned heavily upon intermingling of sexes, and we could never muster up enough courage to approach girls.) So, a bit like Dr Jekyll and Mr Hyde, I had a dual personality. I would be Mr Hyde in college, living it up with scant regard for college rules, but at home I would go about methodically solving problems designed to make even the most intelligent of people think they were morons.

Finally the D-day arrived. We had chemistry and physics on the first day of the JEE. I did chemistry very well. But physics? I believe I solved every problem correctly. I was elated. The next day was a different story, though. I did badly in math and briefly considered dropping out. But encouraged by a close friend, I completed the last exam, English.

I blissfully forgot all about the IITs after that and focused on preparing for the State Engineering Entrance Exam. This was great fun, since I enrolled in a coaching centre to while away my time, get hold of tonnes of practice questions and admire the beautiful girls who also attended classes at the centre (in the reverse order of importance). I was highly successful in the last part and would sit on the last bench from where I had an unhindered view of everyone in class. A few weeks later, early one morning while I was preparing to leave the house for the entrance exam for the state engineering colleges, our neighbour and my father's assistant came running excitedly with the newspaper in hand. It had the results of the JEE. I quickly dug out my registration number and checked whether it was on the list at all.

I was stunned and completely zapped out of my wits—I had managed to secure the 129th rank. That was 129th in all of India in an exam which 2,00,000 students had taken and which about a million more had not even attempted because it was too tough.

That day, I was on cloud nine. I felt like an otter which had just received a lifetime supply of fish.

Incredibly, the whole examination centre for the state entrance knew about my performance in the IIT JEE. I was an instant celebrity. For my family, this was a matter of great pride, especially for my father, whose stance regarding our education stood vindicated.

Buoyed by my success, I mustered up some serious courage, and, with a quaking heart, went and told Dolly (a false name I have employed—wisely, I believe—to ensure that her husband does not come baying for my blood), a girl on whom I had a huge crush, that I was madly in love with her. Nothing wrong with this, of course, except that it was the third time and the longest sentence I had ever spoken to her.

She was quite sweet and mature about it. She politely pointed out to me that we were too young to think about mad love and so on, and that I should focus on going off to IIT and building a great future. She also wished me all the best. Miffed and hurt, I walked away.

I learned two things...

1. No problem is unsolvable. If one puts one's mind to it and approaches it from all angles, any problem can be cracked.
2. It is incredibly stupid to tell a girl you are madly in love with her if you have only ever spoken three sentences to her.

2. English-speaking, West-loving Metro Types

I joined up for a B.Tech. (Electronics) at IIT Madras in 1985. I was only sixteen, thanks to overenthusiastic parents who had admitted me to school at the age of four. My first time in the institute was daunting. From back-of-beyond villages and small towns, I had come to a metropolis. This was only the second time I had left Kerala, and on the earlier occasion four years previously, I had been so scared of my English-speaking cousins with whom I was staying that I had thrown up in their car, a memory which made me hate this city (and one which must have made them think of me as a dimwitted country bumpkin).

Worse, I had never ever held a conversation in English before and was petrified to speak in that language (a fact I hid behind the veneer of reverse snobbery and contempt for the capitalistic English-speaking, West-loving metro types). The number of Malayalis in undergraduate IIT courses was small, and the few who were there were mainly from outside Kerala. Worse, their preferred medium of communication was English—a fact which made me

15

think more poorly of them than of the metro-type non-Malayalis.

My dad had sent my brother BalG—just two years older than me—to settle me down in the hostel. It was his way of helping both of us grow up. It was an interesting two days, in which both of us together discovered how to buy a second-hand cycle, a second-hand fan, a brand new mini drafter (a somewhat weird-looking equipment which engineers used to whip out at the drop of a hat to start drawing parallel lines) and a bucket and a mug. We also experimented with our first few sentences in English. It must have been an equally, if not more, daunting two days for BalG. He must have suffered from the same mental demons as me—inferiority complex, struggle with English and lack of familiarity with the place. In addition, he had to pretend to be in total control to give me confidence. I think he did an amazing job for an eighteen-year-old.

Finally, the day arrived when BalG had to go back. That evening, I went to Madras railway station to drop him. He got into the coach and the train started to move. That was when the realization dawned on me that he was leaving me alone in this English-speaking, unfamiliar world, and that I had to fend for myself from then on. I felt utterly lonely, and tears sprang to my eyes and streamed down my cheeks. That night, Madras station witnessed the strange sight of a sixteen-year-old boy walking down the platform, looking completely woebegone, with tears streaming down his face, while an eighteen-year-old craned his neck out of a departing train, feeling terrible at the sight of his brother crying, and feeling miserable for leaving him all alone.

In the next few weeks, IIT descended on me like a tonne of bricks. The place seemed to be crawling with seniors. As any smart IITian would tell you, since B.Tech. is a four-year course, the chances of bumping into a senior are three times as high as bumping into a fresher. Since freshers generally tried to blend into the surroundings to avoid detection, the chance of bumping into seniors was even higher. Consequently, I was ragged half a dozen times each day. Ragging—for those of you who may be clueless—is a barbaric, cultish practice, prevalent in those days in most colleges, of seniors ganging up and insulting the juniors and often making them do funny stuff with the express purpose of humiliating them. (This is a bit similar to hazing that happens in American universities.) My lack of expertise in English and my atrocious Malayali accent were always the butt of the worst form of ragging.

The ragging, even though hurtful at times, was usually quite friendly. One senior in particular, Sandeep Sibal, helped me tremendously. He noticed that I generally moved around with another Malayali classmate of mine. At the end of a ragging session, he told me, 'You have come to a completely new place, and this place is completely cosmopolitan. You need to choose whether you want to stick to your Mallu (Malayali) friends or mix with others and learn a lot.'

This advice changed my life. I decided to give the non-Malayalis a chance to prove their worthiness to me. In fact, I went a step further. Just to cure myself of my Malayali-friend addiction, I decided to undergo a cold turkey treatment. I consciously stayed off Malayalis. As a result, I had no option but to hobnob with the others; and, wonder of wonders, I realized that these guys were not too bad after all.

I realized that these people also owed their allegiance to the Constitution of India and not to that of the USA. Most of them believed in equality, were not casteist and respected other religions. Most important, they spoke English because they were brought up in cosmopolitan surroundings where English was the only common medium of communication and not because they wanted to put down sons of the soil like me.

From being a reverse snob who looked down upon everything not genuinely Malayali, I became an active seeker of diversity. I started absorbing, understanding and enjoying cultures, cuisines and viewpoints which were different from mine.

I learned two things…

1. If you push yourself out of your comfort zone, you will grow as a person. A corollary is that unless you push yourself out of your comfort zone, you cannot grow as a person.
2. Tandoori chicken and roti are every bit as good as fish curry and rice.

---

3. The IIT Lingo

Anthropology tells us that when any civilization gets cut off from the rest of the world for a longish period of time, it usually develops a new language. It was the same in the case of IIT Madras, a 500-acre nerd island in the middle of the city. Any study of the culture and history of IIT is incomplete without a thorough understanding of this language and its roots. I must at this juncture confess to my readers that I do not claim to have done a Ph.D in the subject but am merely someone who has made extensive use of it. The IITian also lacks an official script, which has prompted some experts to relegate it to the level of a mere dialect. I am opposed to any such ridiculous move. I have tried to give here some of the most commonly used words and phrases and my assessment of their meanings and origins.

Ass wardy: Other than the President of India, this is possibly the most honorary and powerless position in the universe. It is awarded to a teaching assistant or a Ph.D student for the sole purpose of ensuring the occupation of the large room with an attached bathroom next to the common room in each of the twelve hostels in IIT. The fact that the ass wardy is also known as the assistant warden of the hostel remains a well-kept secret.

Arbit: This word is quite versatile in the sheer magnitude of meanings that it could cover. It could equally mean 'out of the ordinary', 'less than desirable' or 'off the rocker'. Nowadays this master word has been replaced by a far inferior one: 'random'.

Bugger: This is a common noun and not to be mistaken for the verb form of the same word with a somewhat unsavoury meaning. It means chappie or guy.

Ditch: This is also quite a versatile word which can be used to connote various forms of betrayal, abnegation or rejection. Usage: 'I am ditching the class today. I need to catch up on my sleep' or 'You ditched me, you moron! Couldn't you wait for me?' The other forms of this word are ditchax and ditcha—both of them tending to mean 'Get lost, punk'.

Despo: A person who exhibits characteristics of being desperate for something. For example, one could be called a despo if one is desperate for better grades or, as in the case of all IITians, if one is desperate for female company.

Funda: This word originated from the far less versatile English word 'fundamental'. This could mean intelligence or a person of high intelligence. It could also mean the theory behind anything, for example, 'The funda behind the desponess of IITians is the skewed sex ratio'. The plural of funda is fundae. One can also use a variation, 'fundu', as in 'He is a fundu bugger'.

Muggo: This is what all IITians would like to believe every other IITian is and they themselves are not. It means someone who studies a lot, which is considered passé in IIT since one would rather be a fundu bugger and score marks without studying anything rather than be a muggo.

Oeshed (sometimes referred to also as *ooshed*): This is fully as versatile as the 'F' word and encompasses as many shades of surprise, anguish, anger and fear. It is also used like the word of words as an adjective or an adverb depending on the specific usage. I suspect that the roots of this word are a mix of Tamil and German. The usage could be in as widely varying contexts such as 'Oh I am so ooshed' or 'You ooshed bugger' or 'Oh ooshed'.

Pill: This means to lie, that too brazenly. Usage: 'Hey I pilled to the prof today that I have a stomach ache.'

Potlam: This word is borrowed from Tamil and translates as 'a small packet', an innocuous enough word. However, the contents of the small packet are what give it considerable significance. A potlam typically contains grass (or weed as it is known nowadays). The grading and hence the pricing of the above-mentioned content depends on its source, Velachery (a village adjacent to IIT) potlam being of the lowest quality and the one from the hill station of Thekkadi having the highest quality stamp.

Quark: A very fundamental component of IIT life. This was an open-air cafe that served palatable food to the starving IITians whose only other source of food would be the mess. The groups of concrete blocks strewn around the quark were perfect meeting places for students who wanted to lick their wounds after a particularly difficult mid-term exam or for holding birthday parties. A place I used to haunt multiple times a day to grab a smoke and down a cup of tea. The delicacies here included tea or coffee at Re 1 or cheese toast at Rs 3. At the beginning of the month, when we had some extra disposable income, we could afford a bun omelette at Rs 5 or a cheese omelette at Rs 10. The height of luxury was the pizza for Rs 15 which had to be invariably shared with three to ten others.

Supie: A title bestowed on an official-looking bloke whose only occupation in life, apparently, was to sit at one end of the mess hall and sell coupons for extras such as curd, non-vegetarian dishes, eggs, etc. In antiquity, the supie was also known as the supervisor.

Tharams: The other place of solace for the starving IITians escaping the wrath of the mess. The variety available here was much broader, ranging from dosas to bun omelettes. The fact that the entire village was as filthy as a pigsty did not in any way deter us from multiple visits a day.

Thon: A derogatory term for Malayalis. The Malayali was easily spotted in IIT because of (a) his thick moustache and (b) his thick accent.

Vague rice: This is a carbohydrate concoction of unknown composition which was dished out with amazing regularity in every hostel for dinner on Tuesdays. In some hostels where the supie was particularly sadistic, the vague rice was dished out twice a week. The effect of consuming the vague rice was to instantly instill in the consumer a deep hatred for humanity.

Vels (pronounced vales): IIT's neighbouring territory, officially referred to as Velachery by outsiders. Its only claim to fame was the availability of the above-mentioned potlam.

I learned two things...

But they come under the heading of unprintable words and so I need to refrain from sharing them with my readers.

---

4. Deep Dive on the Rollercoaster

IIT was a great place to be in once I had decided that every individual was worthy of my friendship. My social circle widened several times in one fell swoop—so much so that my attention was completely diverted from academic to social matters, such as spending the night prior to an exam playing bridge.

However, what took up progressively more and more of my time were spiritual matters. My favourite spirit was Old Monk rum. A close runner-up was a potent bottled amber liquid which went by the handle of Bullet beer. I am pretty sure that it contained a dash of sulfuric acid and a touch of TNT.

To understand the significance of the above-mentioned spirituality, one should first understand how consuming alcohol was perceived in those days. Unlike people from the West or even Indians today, drinking was considered one of the worst sins by the middle class of that time. Most people of this class who indulged did so surreptitiously. In my household especially, this was considered one of the worst forms of debauchery. My father, who never drank any form of alcohol, was convinced that it was only the morally corrupt and those who made tonnes of money through official corruption who indulged in spirits. So, for me, my spirituality was a huge break from tradition. In some ways, I guess I was rebelling.

My GPA (Grade Point Average: an elaborate rating system designed exclusively to keep me at the bottom of the class) followed a linear curve, starting at 8.5 and dropping half a point each semester. For those mathematically inclined, the equation could be $Y=mX+C$, where 'Y' is the GPA, m = -0.5, 'X' is the semester and 'C' is 9. Inserting an appropriate value of X in this formula, one can easily see that by the sixth semester, my GPA reached 6.0.

From the third semester onwards, we started having core subjects and electives in our department, the Department of Electrical Engineering. According to most students, this was incorrect nomenclature and the actual name should have been Concentration Camp. If all the professors of IIT Madras were stacked one on top of the other in ascending order of toughness, the five at the very top would have all been from our department (though I would have preferred them to be at the bottom of the heap, getting the bejesus squeezed out of them). This high 'tough professor' index obviously caused my GPA to decline further, but it was by no means the only reason.

I have tried to analyse exactly what had happened to me during those days that made me go into this tailspin. It would be easy for me to blame the system and say that the atmosphere in IIT was not nurturing or that the professors did not capture one's imagination. But that would be pure, unadulterated bullshit. The real reason was quite different. I was a nincompoop. Not the IQ-lacking type, but the type who did not think far enough; the type who tried to cultivate a cool dude image; the type who lost focus.

Since I came from a state where Class 11 and 12 were called pre-degree and were part of the university, where one studied along with undergraduate and graduate students, there was complete freedom for students to walk in and out of classes and to bunk as many lectures as one wanted. As I said earlier, in the two years of pre-degree, I must have attended about forty classes.

So in IIT, I realized that my ability to focus and learn in a class was low—I was not able to concentrate. I also thought of myself as someone who could cut classes and still score well. Except that in IIT, if you cut classes, it is extremely difficult to make sense of the subject by yourself. As I cut more classes, the gap in my understanding widened. This led to my losing interest in the subject, which led to more cutting of classes, and so on. I was caught in one vicious downward spiral.

What was worse, as I started tanking academically, I decided to boost my image in other ways. Not being a great sportsman or any sort of an artist, there was only one option open to me—to try and pretend to be a cool dude who did not care. I stepped up my boozing and smoking. (I know what you are thinking. Don't say it. I completely own up to having been a total and unmitigated mutt.)

Life was not completely wasted, of course. I did pick up some special skills. I was the acknowledged campus-wide expert on making punch. I used to get invited from far and wide to make my special punch for parties. The basic ingredients consisted of one bucket of an orange drink called Rasna, two bottles of Old Monk rum, one bottle of gin, half a bottle of vodka and half a bottle of whisky. An extra quarter bottle of rum was an essential part of the overall mix—specifically required to supply me with energy while I mixed the punch.

Another important skill I picked up was how to deliver the pithiest and most impactful expletives in almost all Indian languages and a few foreign ones. As a result, I could easily switch from 'du bist ein schweinhund' to 'mairandi' to 'bokka choda' to even more impactful words while lovingly addressing my best friends.

The third skill which was critical to survival in Madras was that of conserving Dihydrogen Monoxide, also known as water. During summers, water supply was considerably restricted in our hostels. We invented several innovative methodologies to conserve this scarce resource. The first was to brush our teeth with rum. Since our wing mate, Danny, had contacts in the military, it was easy for us to get hold of subsidized liquor. Hence rum was actually more easily available than water. The next measure was to hold rituals called community baths. All of us stood around one single drum and bathed.

Another skill, and possibly the most important of the lot, was the ability to make war. This usually happened during Diwali. We used to have intra-wing, inter-wing and inter-hostel rocket fights. Of these, the most exciting and of course the most stupid were the intra-wing fights, where we would fire rockets at each other from one end of the hostel wing to the other—a distance of some 50 feet.

I learned another invaluable skill from my cousin, Chandrasekhar Vallath, known as Unni. The ability to use humour to keep people engaged. Unni used to visit me at my hostel and keep me and my friends in splits.

Meanwhile, as I stepped on the 'moron pedal', the institute in turn stepped on the 'tough prof pedal'. There was only one, Antony Reddy, in the fourth semester. In the fifth, there were Profs. Rao, Bhatt and Raina. Instead of failing in one subject, I failed in four in the fifth semester. I realized at last with sickening clarity that I might have some difficulty graduating in four years.

What ensued was a desperate scramble for summer courses that one could enrol in to make up some of the credits. There were four other students who were in the same boat, and we went from professor to professor to try and get them to offer summer courses. We finally eked out a couple of them. They were hardly relevant to our programme but helped fill the yawning gap in credits. But it was crystal clear that without these, I would not be able to complete my graduation in four years.

That summer, I stayed back on campus to do a couple of summer courses and try and make up the difference. It was a last-ditch attempt to salvage the situation. It was also a convenient way to avoid meeting my parents. I was very close to them, and it would have been difficult not to reveal my worries to them during a two-month stay.

But I could not put off the meeting indefinitely. During the seventh semester, they came to Madras for a one-week visit. I could never hide my feelings from my mother, and she immediately sensed that there was something wrong. Painfully at first, but then with growing relief, I told my parents what had happened. I expected anger and disappointment. But their reaction was completely unexpected. The only emotion I saw on their faces was deep concern. They just wanted to know how they could help me.

I told them that I really did not need any help; I had just wanted to inform them of the situation; and that I would need their support for one more year of undergraduate study. My father gently suggested that it might be a good idea for him to meet some of my professors. I was alarmed. What all the professors would tell him! But, more than that, I felt bad that my father had to go as a supplicant before my professors because of my stupidity. He gently explained to me that it would not be a loss of face for him and that he was not doing anything that a father would not do for his son.

So, one hot summer day in Chennai, with the temperature hovering around 43^0 C, the two of us walked into my department. My dad patiently met each professor, sometimes going back two to three times because some of them were not available. His message to them was simple: 'We are from a middle class family, and we are all very close. RamG used to love his subjects but has been missing home and has lost focus. He is trying to get back on track. Do support him in this.'

Most of the professors were sympathetic. They immediately identified with the concern and pain of a father and a middle class government employee. That visit at least took away the negativity that the professors must surely have felt towards me and brought me back on a level playing field.

My parents had saved my life. I was filled with gratitude. Of course, today I realize that it was just one of the hundreds of other equally important things they had done for me.

I decided not to break my head trying to graduate in four years. There was an angel in disguise who saved me in the final stage—Dr Prabhu, my project guide. He took me on when no one else was willing to mentor my project. I graduated in five years, with a GPA of 8 in the last two semesters.

By that time, I got admission in the Xavier Labour Relations Institute (XLRI), one of the best management institutes in the country, in Jamshedpur. It was time to write a new chapter.

I learned two things…

1. Never hesitate to reach out to loved and dear ones when in trouble. They will always support you. Equally important, try and help out as many people as possible when they are going through difficulties. You could be saving someone's life.
2. If you mix eight different types of liquor in one night, you are bound to feel like a dead fish with an upset tummy the next day.

5. Rat Race

Having thus escaped suicidal depression by the skin of my teeth, I decided to join the rat race with gusto. Not that I knew too much about what management meant, but I knew that I didn't really stand a chance to either work as an electronics engineer or to do higher studies in electronics: I was out of my depth even after studying the subject for five years.

That was how I landed up at XLRI in 1990 at the age of twenty-two. Apart from being one of the top five management institutes in the country and being the best for human resource management, XLRI had another even more important distinction; it had the best sex ratio of all the premier management institutes in the country.

For me, having come from IIT, where approximately 98 per cent of the students were men, this sudden deluge of the opposite sex was like manna from heaven. What was more, the quality was even more impressive than the quantity. I lost no time in losing my heart, time and again and again and again.

The course itself was a cakewalk. My favourite subjects were economics and quantitative techniques, where I held a huge advantage over most others with my strong quant bias. Organizational behaviour, accounting, marketing, and so on were subjects I had to put up with and pass with decent grades. This I did with relative ease.

I did spread my quant 'fundas' far and wide. Before every quant exam, I ended up taking classes for a very substantial percentage of my class. Quite often, I missed out on a whole night's sleep since I had to cover the entire portion and do it at a pace which would be suitable for the lowest denominator. I enjoyed it thoroughly. I was adding value to someone's life.

My spiritual pursuits only kept increasing in XLRI. Having a retired major from the army as my roommate helped shore up my spirits considerably. At the beginning of each month, he would pick up a dozen bottles of rum from the nearest military canteen. Each bottle was worth about Rs 12, which meant that we had a dozen bottles for the incredible price of Rs 144. What with his knack for making friends and our constant and unceasing devotion to this spirit, all the bottles would be empty within ten days. Thus, each month, we ended up downing about three dozen bottles of rum, of which I must have consumed about a quarter.

There were occasions when the canteen did not have our favourite brand, Old Monk. On those days, we had to be content with buying another brand, which came at an even more ridiculous price of Rs 6 per bottle. I found out later that this particular brand was issued in the army for mules, to encourage them to cart considerable loads up hills. The theory was that a sufficiently sloshed mule would float up faster. Well, it was certainly serving some mules somewhere!

This spiritual pursuit also got me into one of the exclusive clubs in XLRI, which was called OMAXI—short for Old Monk's Association of Xavier Institute. (For those not familiar with the noble drink, Old Monk rum is one of the most popular drinks in the country.) The club's selection procedure and the subsequent anointing ceremony were exciting to say the least. The ceremony took place during the marketing fair each year.

The senior year's Old Monk (the most accomplished toper), along with his four monks and four nuns—the eight heaviest drinkers in the batch—walked down from the fourth floor of the main building, carrying burning crosses, wearing white masks and chanting 'Hail Chief'. Once they reached the ground floor, the Old Monk nominated his successor from the junior batch. The newly anointed Old Monk then nominated his group of monks and nuns. This was followed by the 'oath', in which the Old Monk placed his hand on a skull and swore that he would carry forward the tradition of the group, namely, of remaining pickled for the remainder of the year. The rumour was that this skull belonged to the first ever Old Monk.

Apart from this strong spiritual inclination, what I really took away from the two years at XLRI was an extension of what I had started to understand at IIT: respecting the differences between cultures and people and not judging them on these differences. I also learned not to classify people as Punjabis, Bengalis, Delhiites,

Biharis, etc., but to treat each as an individual. From being a pompous, snobbish Malayali, I had come a long way.

At the end of the two years, it was time for placements. Placement time in a B-school would be the climactic leg of the rat race. It would be typically spread over two weeks. Companies would be invited depending on their desirability (the criteria mostly being how much they paid). The most desirable came on Day 1, the next most desirable on Day 2, and so on.

One could see the students, dressed in all their finery, rushing to attend interviews and group discussions. Representatives of companies would vie with each other to make the first offer so that they got the best candidates, since once someone accepted an offer, he or she would be out of the placement cycle.

As the days progressed, the ones who were left behind without jobs started coming under immense pressure. They would feel unwanted, rejected and inadequate. This was especially the case with toppers who failed to get placed in the first three to four days. I was lucky and got placed on the second day with Titan, a very coveted company despite its low pay.

I learned two things...

1. Life is a long, long innings. There are plenty of opportunities to make up and get back on track even if you falter. Just don't give up hope.
2. Mules have it pretty good in the army.

6. Management Trainee

If there is one period in life which is even more fun than campus days, it is the management trainee period. That year, 1992, there were fifteen of us who were recruited by Titan from across various premier management institutes as management trainees (MTs).

For Titan, it was only the second year since they had started the MT programme, and we were treated like royalty. We spent the first month of our induction in Bangalore. Bangalore had three massive advantages which made it the dream destination for us: First, it was the only city in the entire country which had pubs and where one could get pitchers of freshly brewed beer; second, at that time, Bangalore had a minimum temperature of 5^0C and a maximum temperature of 25^0C; last but not the least, the place was crawling with fashionable chicks.

Fifteen young, carefree persons, who were all earning and hence had disposable income, let loose in the pub city of Bangalore: you can imagine the mayhem we created. Added to this was the fact that we all got along like a house on fire. We were put up in two apartments in a residential building, and these two apartments became the geographies

35

with the highest per capita consumption of liquor in the country.

Every night, we partied till 2 a.m. and then nursed a hangover through the next day's induction, just to party till 2 a.m. the next day, and the day after, and the day after. In a matter of one month, we managed to alienate all the other residents in the apartment block—all well-behaved, middle class families. It finally came to a head after one particularly bingey night when the decibel levels reached a crescendo. The neighbours ganged up, knocked on our door and threatened to call the police.

The head of HR in Titan received a formal complaint the next day from the residents' association, and we were ordered on pain of death to go to its president and tender due apologies. We nominated three from amongst us: two of the sweetest of girls and Niloy, a man who towered over everyone at 6'2" and who was almost as wide as he was tall. The president was a retired wing commander and was extremely amiable, maybe because he did not want to take on 120 kilos of aggressive-looking Bengali.

At the end of the one month of training, we were each assigned a territory. The sales GM, in his infinite wisdom, assigned each of us to a location where we would be least comfortable—the Mumbai girl to Orissa, the Delhi girl to Tamil Nadu and so on. I was assigned to western Uttar Pradesh, and I nearly fell off my chair when I heard that. My expertise in Hindi was very limited—mainly restricted to expletives about mothers and sisters—and here I was to go to the Hindi heartland.

My stint in Uttar Pradesh lasted three months. It consisted of standing behind the counter in franchisee showrooms and selling watches to customers, carrying watches to small towns in rickety buses and selling them to small retailers, and understanding our warehouse operations.

I also did something I am not proud of at all. Company policy allowed us to travel between towns in air-conditioned trains. I used to travel by buses, which would cost about a tenth of the train charge, but shamelessly claim reimbursement for the fare of a train ticket. In those three months, I must have amassed an enormous sum of Rs 10,000 and felt rather proud of it. When the stint in UP got over and I came back to Bangalore, I told this to a friend, Elango, rather proudly. He was a really close friend and told me that he thought I was an idiot for doing stupid things like this. It was at this point that the enormity of my action hit home.

I was raised by an impeccably honest father. He was a government officer and had held some important senior posts, some of which included handling enormous projects and taking decisions on vendor selections which involved huge outlays. If he was even slightly corrupt, he could have made enough money to fund a couple of generations. But he was scrupulously honest. He even refused to use the department car for anything other than official business. For personal use, even while holding very senior positions, he would use his scooter. And here I was, the son of that man, shamelessly making dishonest money. I felt ashamed and guilty. I made up for what I had done by not claiming reimbursements for a few of the subsequent expenses until I was sure that I had returned to the company what I owed it.

From that day to date, I have been impeccably honest in all my dealings.

I learned two things...

1. One's reputation is built slowly and painstakingly, step by step, doing the right thing each time. It takes only one wrong move to destroy that edifice.
2. Never drink a pitcher of beer priced at Rs 37. It is bound to be one day old and hence taste like a baboon's piss (I suspect).

7. Long-Distance Love

The next couple of years proved to be extremely fruitful for me on the personal front. Jayashri, who was a junior at XLRI, joined Titan the next year. We were not romantically involved when we were students, though we were good friends.

But within a month of her joining Titan, after many dinners, long bike rides and heart-to-hearts, I was completely in love.

Unfortunately, at the end of that month, I moved to Hubli (overnight from Bangalore by bus) and she moved to Hosur (couple of hours from Bangalore on the opposite side), and our romance went into long-distance mode. But just before the move, I managed to shove in a proposal, which she quickly accepted.

Those were the days when we actually wrote letters and posted them and waited for the postman to bring replies. We had one more mode of communication: the telephone—not the sleek thingy one carries around in a pocket but a black monstrosity which had a rotary dial. The long distance calls were Rs 32 per minute. Just to put things in perspective, my house rent was Rs 400 for a whole month. So you can imagine how expensive it was to listen to the voice of a loved one. However, the department of telephones had an extremely sporting offer for the love-struck youth. After 10 p.m., the rate for long-distance calls would dramatically fall to Rs 4 per minute. Since I did not have a phone at home (only near-royalty had phones at home in those days), I would finish dinner and call Jayashri (Jayu) from the nearest phone booth.

Since she also did not have a phone at home, she had to take these calls from a neighbour's house. A slight complication arose when the ringer in the neighbour's phone went dead. But long-distance love is highly innovative and we found a solution to the problem. Every day, at exactly 10 p.m., she would start picking up the receiver and placing it back. Since we had synchronized our watches, chances were high that she would pick up the receiver right when I was calling her.

The real challenge lay in telling our respective parents about our proposed matrimony. Jayu, who was born and brought up in Mumbai, belonged to a Tamil Brahmin family. I belonged to a Malayali Menon family.

You might think that we are all 'South Indians' so it's no big deal. For those of you who are not very familiar with these terms, let me take a minute to explain. In those days, India was almost like twenty-odd different countries, each state with its own culture and language. The Malayalis from Kerala thought of the Tamilians from Tamil Nadu as an inferior species and, amazing as it sounds, the Tamilians felt exactly the same way about the Malayalis.

Apart from this, there was an even bigger complication. Hindu society is divided into many castes and sub castes. Brahmins are the upper caste, while I belonged to a relatively lower caste. So, let me tell you, it was a huge deal. Apart from having different mother tongues, we also belonged to different castes. Our cultures were quite different. The caste and regional biases were so strong in those days (the situation is only marginally better today) that marrying someone from a different caste was heavily frowned upon. It was so bad that Brahmins marrying non-Brahmins could even invite excommunication and shame.

In those days, and even today to a certain extent, weddings were not a matter of personal choice. Weddings were fixed by the families of the girl and the boy. This was done by matching religion and caste, family wealth, education levels of the couple involved, and so on. Marriages fixed by the boy and girl themselves were called 'love marriages' and were frowned upon by civilized society. This was an added complication in our case.

Both Jayu and I waited for a good opportunity to speak to our respective parents.

For me, the moment of truth came about when my father, on his way to Delhi, dropped by in Goa, which was then part of the sales territory I was handling. It was wonderful to see him. After a nice dinner, we retired to the room which we were sharing. My dad switched on the TV to watch a one-day cricket match between India and Pakistan.

Knowing that it would be impossible to get his attention

once the match hotted up, I quickly dived in. In one breath, I told him that there was a lovely girl, Jayashri, that I was in love with and that she was a junior from college and was working with me at Titan. After getting this much out quickly, I expectantly looked at his face.

He asked me one question: 'Is she a Tamilian?' I said yes, and he grimaced and continued watching the match without saying anything further. I was flabbergasted. I had prepared a lot of points witch which to buttress my arguments and to convince him that Jayu was the ideal mate for me. But how does one rebut an argument which has not been butted to start with?

I remember walking out of the room in a huff and calling up Jayu. I bitterly cribbed about heartless parents. Finally I went back to the room and slept, ignoring my dad who was still glued to the TV. The game was a day-and-night match and was being played in Sharjah. This meant that it would go on till about 1 a.m. India time.

Around midnight, I was woken up by an excited dad. India was clawing back from an apparently hopeless position, and Sachin Tendulkar was thrashing the daylights out of the Pakistani bowlers. My dad could not control his excitement. He had to share the moment with someone and had woken me up. This more than anything else is one of the reasons why I am an ardent fan of Sachin's.

India won the match—an incredible victory—and we both slept happily.

Next day, over breakfast and during the ride to the airport, both of us carefully skirted the topic. Finally, just before getting into the boarding area, my dad told me, 'If you are convinced that you want to marry this girl, please go ahead and do it. It is not necessary to involve us (the parents) in the wedding. And, of course, then you might as well also do it in Bangalore or Bombay or any other place of your choice. No need to do this in Kerala.' He obviously was trying to make me feel bad.

I did not rise to the bait. I said, 'No. I will not go ahead with the marriage till you and mom agree to it. I will wait as long as it takes.' I cleverly took the moral high ground and the wind out of his sails.

Within a week of getting back home, my dad wrote me a long letter. In it, he explained why my news of wanting to marry a Tamilian had upset him.

'Even in an arranged marriage, where both the boy and the girl are from the same community and similar backgrounds, where both families wholeheartedly support the wedding, the chances of problems cropping up are high. So in a situation like this, where the differences are many, the chances of the marriage surviving are really low,' he said. 'But if you are really keen on going ahead, please make sure that you get complete support from Jayu's father. If he agrees to the wedding, so will we.'

I understood where he was coming from. He was seeing things from the point of view of someone who had stayed in Kerala all his life. He saw a strong part being played by the families of the couple in the marriage. I realized that there were now considerable differences between my lifestyle and what my parents were used to. I could understand where he was coming from but did not agree with him. But the fact remained that I did not want to get married without the blessings of both sets of parents, and I was willing to wait as long as it took for that to happen. So was Jayu.

I learned two things…

1. Even people with similar values and the same overall vision can have disagreements. It is important at such times to try and understand the other person's point of view and then work towards a win-win situation. A corollary of that is that one can work towards a win-win situation only if one has the patience to understand the other person's point of view.
2. If you are an Indian, do not try to hold any serious discussion while a cricket match is on.

---

8. Hectic Negotiations

The first step now was to get an approval from Jayu's father, whom she called Appa. Her mother had died of Motor Neuron Disease (MND) many years previously at the age of forty-five.

Jayu's first attempt at convincing Appa was a total disaster. It happened when she had gone to stay with Appa in Mumbai during a holiday. One evening, she subtly broached the topic of having a boyfriend. Even before she could complete the sentence, Appa got up from his seat and threatened to jump off the window. Since they were situated on the eleventh floor, and gravity being 9.8 m/s^2 in Mumbai, Jayu had no option but to desist from further discussions on the subject. She went back to Hosur feeling completely let down and all ready to elope.

We had a powwow to reassess the situation and recast our strategy. This was when Jayu came up with the idea of taking the support of her elder sister, Shubha. Then she would talk to Appa and, if required, take Shubha's support in convincing him. He would then in turn convince the grandmother, Jayu's mother's mother, whom she called Patti. All in all, it was an elaborately laid out plan to solve a problem with many variables—that too, mostly random variables.

Shubha was six years older than Jayu, and the two sisters were extremely close. Jayu sat down and wrote a long letter to Shubha, explaining the situation. Shubha was aghast. Jayu had mentioned me several times to her earlier (before we started seeing each other) and had spared no effort in describing me as the right hand of the devil. Now the sudden and complete U-turn took Shubha by surprise. But Jayu arranged a face-to-face meeting, and I went down extremely well with not only Shubha but also her husband Ananthakrishnan (Nandu for short).

Shubha started nibbling away at Appa's resistance, and finally he agreed to grant me an audience.

Thus I landed in Mumbai, full of apprehension and anticipation to make first contact. The chosen location was Shubha's house. I was to stay there for two days and Appa was to land up during daytime to hobnob with me and assess my viability. Originally, Jayu was also supposed to come with me, but her plan got scuttled since there was a lockout in the Titan factory and she was part of the HR team handling the situation.

So, there I was, bearding the lion in his den (or in his daughter's den, strictly speaking), without even the support of the one who had shoved me in there.

That fateful day, I waited in Shubha's house for Appa to descend, with a heart full of apprehension and hope. And his first words as he descended were: 'So Jayu's trip has gone f****d?'

I goggled at him, aghast and impressed. I had no idea that he spoke my type of language.

'So Jayu's trip has gone phut?' he asked again, his kind, humorous eyes twinkling.

Ah! I realized he had said 'phut', meaning 'kaput', and not the word of words.

Even though it turned out that he did not use my type of words, over the next couple of days I came to the conclusion that he was a decent bloke—quite amiable and sweet, though he did take me through a bit of history (namely, from his own childhood to adulthood) in excruciating detail. By the end of two days, we were on decidedly chummy terms.

I must confess that I did employ some slightly underhand methods to gain his love. While studying at IIT Madras, I had heard some Karnatik devotional songs being sung by classmates. Though I was not majorly into Karnatik, I remembered snatches from a couple of them. I made it a point to hum and sing these whenever Appa was in the vicinity. He was duly impressed. Anyone who could sing 'Swaminatha Paripalayam' and 'Bantureethi Kolu' couldn't be all bad. I could see that he had started warming up to me. The IIT factor helped, though my fifth year in IIT was conveniently omitted.

Let me expound a bit on why the IIT background helped. Of course, an IIT background generally helps, but in the Tamil Brahmin community, it helps extraordinarily. The aspiration of all Tamil Brahmin parents is to have their children eventually go to the USA, which they consider the land of milk and honey. And IIT is considered the best way to reach the land of M&H. This is why you will find a massive number of Tamil Brahmins infesting IITs. So when Appa heard that I am from IIT, he must have thought to himself that I am almost a Tamil Brahmin.

Even though our chats were going along great, my restlessness kept growing, since, even after forty-eight hours, the gentleman never once mentioned the holy alliance between his daughter and yours truly. I felt a bit deflated, much like what Pervez Musharraf must have felt when, after being invited by Bill Clinton to discuss a $1-billion aid, at the end of the visit he discovered that all he and Bill had discussed was Pakistani women, cigars, terrorists, kababs and what not.

But I was made of stronger stuff. In the last five minutes before I was to eject from the house, I took courage in both hands and, with a prayer in my heart, told him: 'Uncle, I am sorry if I have hurt you in any way by falling in love with your daughter.' Impressive stuff, you must admit. And it finally penetrated the armour. He got quite emotional, and I could see that I was now well on the way to winning the trophy.

Now all Appa had to do was bell the cat, or rather, beard the lioness; meaning, he had to break the news to the grandmother. It must have been a tough task. But then Appa was far tougher than one would give him credit for. On the face of it, he was a quintessential Tamil Brahmin— god-fearing, honest, completely risk-averse, and so on. (He was the type who would check his ticket seventeen times before leaving for a train journey, then reach the station two hours early and wait on the platform rather than miss it due to, say, an unexpected tornado.) But don't make the mistake of thinking he was a coward.

His wife had been diagnosed with Motor Neuron Disease at forty. They had two daughters aged ten and seventeen at that time. I have heard that he never let hope fade but kept trying all possible remedies he could afford. She passed away within five years of being diagnosed with this incurable disease. I believe that in her last days, he never left her side. She was incapable of doing anything for herself. But he would patiently and smilingly take care of her every need, including getting up in the middle of the night many times to turn her from side to side. Through all this, he ensured that he educated both his daughters. He had no qualms about sending them far away to study. One became an MBA from XLRI and the other got an outstanding rank in the civil services exam.

I heard later that on hearing of Jayu's romance, the grandmother—Patti—mauled Appa. She had a special corner for Jayu, since she had been almost like a mother to her when her mother was unwell and later after she passed away. But after the initial mauling, she grudgingly told him to do what was best.

In the meanwhile, my dad had also met Shubha and Nandu and liked them very much. Subsequently, my parents, BalG and his wife Sonia gave Jayu a surprise visit in Hosur, a test she passed with flying colours.

It was at this time that Jayu and I upped the ante. I had been transferred to Pune as area sales manager and Jayu quit her job and joined a company in Pune.

The prospect of his daughter indulging in unspeakable acts before marriage galvanized Appa into action. He went down to Trivandrum to meet my parents. He took along a cousin for moral support. Not to be outdone, my parents got my grandmom to be present at the summit. Thus armed with heavyweights on both sides, they met.

According to Jayu, Appa was quite a karadi (bear). But luckily, his karadi-ness was reserved exclusively for his daughters. To the rest of the world, he was full of milk and honey. Well, my dad was no less a karadi and, unlike Appa, he distributed his brand of karadi-ness far and wide. The two of us waited with bated breath for news of the summit between the two karadis.

We need not have worried. The sheer sweetness of Appa was so strong that everyone, including my grandmother, was hugely impressed. He was humble, sweet, impressive and god-fearing and came across as a wonderful human being. He, on his part, was quite impressed by my parents, their values and the respect they bestowed on him. So the summit was a resounding success. I would not be too far off the mark if I were to say they all hugged, kissed and whooped in happiness.

I learned two things…

1 Just because a person is mild-mannered does not mean that he or she is weak. In fact, the ability to be mild-mannered is a strength in itself.

2. Never get your prospective father-in-law started on his life story without first slyly stuffing your ears with cotton. Just remember to nod every time he closes his mouth.

9. Wedding Bells

The wedding now had to be planned. Should it be a Tamil Brahmin–style wedding or a Malayali Menon–style wedding? Usually this is the point at which most interstate wedding plans come to a screeching halt. Usually there are questions like: Should the attendees drink themselves silly or restrict themselves to buttermilk? Should there be four varieties of fish served or should the feast be pure vegetarian? Should the groom arrive on a horse or should he have pappadam broken on his head? Should the bride sit in her father's lap (ouch!) or should she sit on his shoulder (double ouch!!)? These and other such intricate questions have troubled India's brave interstate couples since time immemorial. The normal practice would be for families to draw themselves up, snort snobbishly and take strong positions such as: 'How dare they not allow pappadam to be broken on his head? This marriage cannot happen', or 'No fish curry on the day of the wedding? My relatives will think we are marrying beggars'.

Luckily, since I was not a Brahmin, it sort of ruled out the Brahmin-style wedding. Menial mortals were not eligible for that. This meant the wedding would be in

Kerala. This also meant Appa would be spared from placing Jayu in his lap.

Usually, in most communities in India, it is the bride's family which hosts the wedding. Then the groom's side holds a reception so that things are generally even-steven. The bride's father gets to show off his immense wealth and good taste by decorating the bride in a few kilos of gold, while the groom's dad gets to indulge in some one-upmanship by hiring the best hall in the best five-star hotel. Unfortunately, in many communities, it is also quite common for the groom's side to insist that the bride be decorated in tonnes and tonnes of gold. This gold is nothing but a form of dowry which my entire family abhorred.

Now, since in this case the wedding was to be in Kerala, my father offered to organize the wedding. Appa was extremely grateful but insisted that he would pay for it in advance and pay any balance after the wedding. He asked my dad how many millions he should send in advance. After careful calculation, my father told him that Rs 20,000 seemed to be a good round sum. I believe Appa swooned at this and had to be revived with a strong dose of rasam. My father's explanation was simple. In our family, we believed in complete simplicity. So he wanted the wedding to happen in a temple instead of a star hotel. The lunch would be a traditional affair. So the total cost—which would basically be the cost of a couple of garlands, a small contribution to the temple, a traditional lunch for the guests, many banana leaves (on which food was traditionally served), and so on—would not be very high.

Finally, he also made a suggestion: 'In our family, we don't like gold too much. So it would be great if the bride does not wear any gold. And the simplest possible bridal dress would be fine.'

Appa was a simple man, but even for him this seemed altogether too simple. His overall love for the Mallu clan went up substantially. Mallus, whom he had imagined to be blood-sucking leaches who moreover spoke with a horrible accent, suddenly seemed like decent blokes (albeit with the horrible accent intact).

At this juncture, it is important to understand what a Tamil wedding typically is like. The most important thing to remember about a typical Tamil Brahmin wedding is that it is an almost continuous series of tortures which blend seamlessly into each other in such a way that those undergoing the ordeal come out of it feeling completely dazed, headachey, sapped of energy and absolutely in no condition to enjoy the first night or several subsequent nights. My guess is that this is wisely designed on purpose so that the couple is at their lowest in terms of spirit when they start their married life. Then they see it improving each day and attribute this euphoria to being married.

To put the entire thing in a nutshell, the whole process starts with the entry of the groom in a process step—a ceremony, if you will—titled Jana Vasam. This happens on the day prior to the wedding. The groom usually comes from a temple, and the roads are lined with gawking, cheering crowds to ensure the groom is completely embarrassed.

The next day starts with a series of pujas in a hall. This is followed by Vratam, in which the bride and groom are placed separately in front of their respective fires and smoked till they lose any semblance of resistance while the priest keeps feeding ghee into the fire. Usually by then, the groom is totally pained by the proceedings and gets up and runs off on a pilgrimage. This make-believe scooting is called Kasiyatra, or the pilgrimage to the holy city of Kasi. But before the guy can bolt, the bride's father jumps on him and drags him back. Now the bride's father, being highly suspicious of the groom's intentions, corners the groom's father and makes him promise to have the son delivered. This part of the proceedings is called Vaaku Nichayam: giving one's word.

Having completed this, garlands are exchanged. Then both the bride and groom are supposed to sit together on a swing, oonchhal, and sing to each other. And no, the groom cannot subtly squeeze the bride during this proceeding.

By this time, the couple is reasonably exhausted. To pep up the situation, the groom is given a foot massage, the lucky pig. It is at this juncture that the bride plonks herself down in her father's lap and is ceremonially handed over to the groom.

Around this time, the bride and groom move into a trance and become blissfully oblivious to the many more pujas and mantram+ghee that happen around them. There is a weak attempt at a later stage to revive them by making them play some games, which is quickly quelled again by another series of pujas. Sometime during this, the bride has to kick a grindstone (without shoes on, at that!), look at constellations, and get showered by grains. In between all this, the groom is also given the bride's hand to hold, and he is officially allowed to squeeze her hand.

By the time the first night happens, the bride and groom in all probability would have consumed a couple of aspirins and be pleading for mercy. Consummating the marriage would be the last thing on their minds.

In Jayu's family, they go one step further and the groom is made to visit three temples and dance to Lord Murugan before he can jump into bed.

Now in contrast to this is the Mallu wedding. The bride and groom enter the temple; the bride's hand is given to the groom to hold together with a betel leaf within five minutes of entering; he squeezes her hand happily; they walk around a lit lamp a few times and are declared man and wife. Then they are fed milk and banana to shore up their energies to proceed with more exciting stuff.

Our wedding took place on 5 February 1995 in Ernakulam at the temple near our house. Jayu looked stunning in her traditional silk sari. The visiting Tam Brahm clan, which must have come prepared for a two-days-of-smoke-and-fire-which-cause-headache kind of a wedding, felt as if the rug was pulled from under their feet when, after being herded into the temple, after the first blink, they were told that RamG and Jayu were now officially man and wife.

They must have collectively muttered, 'Cheated, I say,' in their proper Tamil accents.

Anyway, the deed was done.

Appa had carried about Rs 50,000 in cash with him to give my father after the wedding. He was sure the Rs 20,000 he had given earlier would not in any way suffice for the expenses. He hesitantly went up to my father and said politely, 'Sir, I would like to pay the balance if you can tell me how much I owe you.'

My father pulled out a sheet in which a detailed item-by-item calculation had been done. He handed it to Appa and said, 'Sir, this is a detailed account of how I have spent the money entrusted to me. As you can see, I have managed to save about Rs 1,632 from that. Please take this back.' So saying, he handed over Rs 1,632 back.

Appa was completely stunned. Prior to meeting me or my parents, he had always assumed that Malayalis were grasping and money-minded. That my father insisted on a simple wedding, saved from the advance of Rs 20,000 and returned the balance, and insisted that there was no need for Jayu to wear any gold—all of this made him realize how wrong he had been to generalize.

At the same time, my father, who did not think much of Tamilians and had a general vague bias against them, was completely floored by all of them, especially Appa, Shubha and Nandu.

After the ceremony, I went up to Appa and told him, 'Uncle, from now on, I will call you Appa.'

Appa was a very emotional person. His eyes welled up.

'Appa' meant 'father'. The fact that I wanted to call him 'father' and not 'father-in-law (mama)' touched him deeply. For the first time, he hugged me—the first of many, many more times to follow.

I learned two things...

1. If people are willing to let go of the belief that their own culture is the best, they will be able to appreciate the beauty of cultures which are different from their own.
2. Get married to Mallus; you can finish the whole process in ten minutes.

10. Up, Up and Away

After close to six years at Titan, I finally decided to jump ship. Titan was a great company, and I had learned a lot. I had had a very successful stint in sales and got some good exposure in marketing. But the fact remained that Titan's salary in those days made even peanuts look like luxury items.

I moved to Compaq Computer Corporation, at that time a small thirty-man organization in India. Coincidentally, Niloy, my close friend from Titan, also joined Compaq along with me.

Compaq's salary was good by any standards. Consequently, I ended up with a 200 per cent increase in salary (for the mathematically challenged: this meant that my salary grew three-fold). The luxury did not end there. All Compaq employees stayed in five-star hotels while travelling. The office itself was based in a couple of suites in Taj Mansingh in Delhi. On the day Niloy and I joined, we had to travel to Delhi, and both of us had a separate Mercedes to pick us up, courtesy the hotel. Life had taken a huge leap into the kind of luxury I had never imagined before.

If Titan was a great place to learn the basics of sales and marketing, Compaq was a fantastic place for learning of a totally different kind: how to build a plane and fly it at the same time (figuratively speaking, of course).

With thirty people in the team, delivering business worth Rs 800 crore ($200 million in those days), each individual had to stretch like crazy. And in my division—the consumer division—the stretch was even more pronounced. The total number of people in the team was four: the head of the business; Ravi Swaminathan, his executive assistant; and two regional managers, Niloy and I, who had then just joined.

Our job was to ensure that the Compaq Presario range of home computers sold through high-profile retail outlets—which we had to set up—and also through the traditional computer reseller channel, whose prime business was to sell business computers to enterprises.

Ravi was one of the most aggressive persons I had ever met, a cross between a dragon and a porcupine, mixed with a lot of humour and loads of magnetism. Moreover, he seemed to have taken an online course from a charging bull. He was an MBA from IIM Ahmedabad and had started his career at Imperial Chemical Industries (ICI), an established paints company, which was very traditional and where business grew 5-10 per cent per annum. It had retained its old British culture, and by the time he quit after seventeen years, he had become a general manager—a very, very senior position. Knowing ICI culture, this meant that he must have been treated like a king, with a massive team of personal secretaries, assistants and yes-men to do all his bidding.

From that position, he had plunged into a completely new sunrise industry. I assume that the first time he touched a computer must have been after he joined Compaq. And he had to work as an individual contributor, with not even one person reporting to him for nearly three years before he had the luxury of two additional headcounts. He became a role model for me in a lot of ways.

The Compaq experience was completely new for me. My responsibility was to ensure that the Compaq Presario range of computers sold very well in south India. The sum total of the information I had from my boss included the names of our five distributors, the contact numbers and names of the owners of three large showrooms (one in Bangalore, one in Chennai and one in Hyderabad) and a list of what our products were. He also suggested a couple of people who could help me learn a bit more about the products (a bit more meant everything about the products except their model numbers, namely, 2801, 2602 and 4401).

Have you ever been dropped in the middle of the ocean from a helicopter? If you have not, imagine how you would feel. Then imagine that you do not know how to swim. What I went through then approximated that experience somewhat. I had to first learn how to swim and then cross the ocean. In other words, I had to learn the basics of computer technology, then learn about our products, then learn about the products of our competition, then dig around and find out who the branch heads of our distributors were, then understand through them who our resellers were, then understand how to increase the sales. This was mostly what a new employee in any organization had to do—except for one massive difference. In most organizations, there are people who would help you understand each of these steps and handhold you. In Compaq's consumer team, there was no one except Ravi, whose inputs, as I stated earlier, were limited to ten names.

To me, this was a problem to be solved, and if you recall, I loved solving problems. I decided to go after each of the problems one by one. I also identified the path of least resistance. The first step would be to meet as many stakeholders as possible, namely, the showroom owners, the resellers, the distributor branch heads, and so on. Compaq had a commercial PC team (ten times the size of the consumer PC team), which had a counterpart of mine. He was the south regional manager for commercial PCs, while I was the regional manager for consumer PCs. I requested him a few times to introduce me to the common channels: the distributor branch managers and the resellers (the relationship with these resellers was 'owned' by him since they were primarily meant for selling commercial PCs to enterprises and not consumer PCs to enterprises). Each time I asked him for help, the answer was a curt 'I am too busy'. I was also moved from my original seat with the sales team to another one next to the secretaries and the operations team (a group of contract employees).

After waiting for a couple of days, I decided to take

matters into my own hands. I called up every distributor branch manager in each of the states and fixed up appointments to meet them. They were more than happy to meet me. Finally, here was someone who could help them address their Presario issues.

What followed was exhilarating. Each branch manager treated me like a long lost brother. Presario always had a product pull among the elite. Unfortunately, the distributors had no idea whom to go to for any kind of information on the product or for any product support. Now they had RamG to go to. I also gave them all my mobile number. (In those days, mobile phones were super luxury items and most people did not like to be disturbed on their mobile phones). I had some rules when it came to mobile phones. I would answer any call within three rings, irrespective of the time and place. If by any chance I could not, I would call back as soon as I saw the missed call. Similarly, an hour was the maximum time I allowed myself to respond to an email. If I couldn't give a satisfactory solution in an hour, I would still respond, asking for more time.

What I realized was that in professional life (and otherwise too), people like to be treated with courtesy and respect. The single most important way of demonstrating it is to be responsive. My channel partners—distributors, retailers and resellers—loved me for it. Within three months, I had as strong a relationship with all key channel partners as the one my counterpart had—sometimes stronger.

Every distributor branch manager became my ally in my quest for channel expansion. They would find potential dealers for me who could become Compaq showrooms. They would actively push the resellers to position Presario products for all requirements (even when the need was for commercial PCs). I ended up setting up thirty Compaq showrooms in two years, the most visible being a showroom bang on MG Road in Bangalore, with a frontage (and a glow signboard) of 72 feet—a retailer's dream.

Another advantage I had was my complete lack of an ego. I must thank my small-village, socialist background for this. By treating the distributors' and resellers' sales persons as equals, I earned their respect, which gave me another huge strategic advantage.

In fact, this huge advantage was also partly due to a perceived 'downfall' from my high-profile table to the one next to the Ops team. Within a couple of months, I had become extremely friendly with all the Ops assistants. (I strongly continue to deny any allegations that this had anything to do with the fact that they were an all-women team!)

The value of this relationship building became apparent over the next few months. Every month, we—the consumer team—had to achieve our monthly revenue targets. These were calculated on the basis of how many dollars worth of computers we could sell to the distributors. Each of these distributors had a credit line from Compaq. This credit line was shared by the consumer PC business and the commercial PC business and was never sufficient for achieving the targets of both businesses together. The credit was released for those orders which were logged in first. My friends in the Ops team made sure that the consumer PC orders were logged in first every single time. I also learned to step way beyond the boundaries of my job. Since we could make a sale to the distributor only after we received consignments by sea from Singapore, it was imperative that the consignments reached our warehouse before the end of the month. I would chase the freight forwarder and the customs clearing agents to ensure that all our consignments reached on time. This job was actually that of the operations team, which would be incredibly busy during month-ends. They were happy and grateful to get a helping hand. As for me, I felt a lot more relieved to be controlling the situation. So we achieved our targets every month, month after month, and I played an important role in this. The only thing I did to facilitate this? I treated all others as equals and gave them the respect they deserved.

Ravi, who had originally been dismayed at not finding me 'aggressive' enough (a conclusion he arrived at because of my meek acceptance of the so-called inferior workstation), actually told me in one of his weaker moments that he realized that aggression is not about thumping the table and talking in a loud voice; it is about going after something tenaciously and believing one's job has no boundaries. My counterpart in the commercial PC side, Anand, was also gracious enough to give Ravi glowing feedback about me.

In the two years I was in Compaq, I got four salary hikes. In effect, within two years, it reached five times the salary I was drawing at Titan.

I learned many things…

1. Any so-called disadvantage can be used as a springboard and turned into an advantage.
2. The only way to build a successful relationship is by respecting the other individual. This means a relationship of equals. This means being responsive to the other's needs.
3. Respect cannot be demanded. It does not come automatically by virtue of your high salary, your cabin or the size of your car. Respect has to be earned.
4. Travelling in a Mercedes is awesome. Staying in a five-star hotel sort of sucks after the first few times.

11. Greed Comes Before a Fall

I was sitting pretty in Compaq. I was achieving my targets; I had a fantastic boss and had an excellent equation with him; I loved my co-workers; they loved me in return; the business was growing at breakneck speed—and that's when I decided to quit.

Reasons: a 50 per cent jump in salary and a national level job in 3Com, a networking hardware MNC. Ravi matched the offer within twenty-four hours but I had already made up my mind to move. I moved to 3Com as all-India distribution head in 1999.

Networking meant loads of technology. I was supposed to sell Ethernet switches, hubs and routers. There was only one small glitch. I did not know what Ethernet was. (I even learned to spell the term with great difficulty.) Selling watches and consumer PCs to unsuspecting resellers does not equip you with knowledge of more esoteric stuff like Ethernet, data switching, TCPIP, etc. (An education in electronics in IIT usually does, but clearly not in my case.)

3Com in India was an even leaner organization than Compaq. The total team strength was of about nine. Of these, eight were for the enterprise business and one—me—for the channel distribution business.

The person I was replacing was a great guy, and we had an overlap of three days. In those three days, he took me around and introduced me to key channel partners and distributors. But what I valued most was the long car drives between offices of channel partners. It was in those long drives that I completely sucked all technical knowledge out of him. I was like a zombie, eating his brains with relish.

I started by confessing that I knew absolutely zilch about the technology and the products. That helped, because he started from absolute ground level. By the end of the third day, I knew quite a bit about the technology, all about each and every current product, the past products and the future product roadmap.

The next month, I actually conducted a training programme for about a hundred resellers. They seemed to enjoy it. I choose to believe it was not the thought of free drinks at the end of the session that kept them going.

Of all the ups and downs I have experienced in life, 3Com was the steepest rollercoaster—up and down.

In the first quarter after I joined 3Com, I launched a blitzkrieg of a promotion. I travelled like a madman, met all distributors and large resellers in the country and, most important, kept my phone on 24x7. This was the first time there was so much excitement for the channels and the first time they felt so supported. That quarter, the distribution business in India did record sales—the highest ever in the history of 3Com India. I was on top of the world. ROFL!

The week after that, 3Com announced a complete restructuring of the company worldwide. It spun off a business into a separate company, closed down half of the rest, reduced product offering in the rest, and came down from $6 billion worldwide to $2 billion.

The following week, my boss, the country manager of 3Com, announced that he was moving out. The company was now two separate entities—3Com and Commworks—and I was officially the head and country manager of 3Com India, handling India and the SAARC region. I also ended up with a 25 per cent salary hike, which meant that in two and a half years, my salary had increased ten-fold. The euphoria of the fancy designation and the fancy salary could not hide the fact that I was in effect left holding a very sick baby.

The customers were pissed off no end about our closing down of product lines. There were IT managers who had trusted the brand and invested in 3Com products. They were now sitting with egg on their faces, because if they wanted to expand their LAN facilities, there was no product offering from 3Com. We had committed the most cardinal of sins; we made our customers look foolish.

The next two years were again for me a period of intense learning. I learned how to cope with customers and channels who thought we were finished as a company. I also learned how to start thinking strategically as a country manager. The first meeting I had with the Asia Pacific head was a disaster. I spoke like a raw front-line sales guy. Luckily, I received feedback that I had screwed up. The next time he came, I put up a thought-through presentation, full of market insights and end-to-end strategy. I had learned.

I also used the one marketing tool which was completely free: PR. Over the next few months, I became a regular contributor to all the industry magazines and IT channel magazines. I also kept up my 24x7 availability to channel partners. Slowly but surely, we gained back some credibility. We would never match Cisco again, but we were no longer a write-off.

Finally, after two years, we won the most prestigious order—that of the National Stock Exchange building.

But, overall, I realized that 3Com was not a good long-term prospect. Even though I was outwardly always cheerful and one to roll up my sleeves and attack problems, my mind would dwell a lot on how to solve each problem. And the two-year stint at 3Com had got me way more stress than I had wanted.

It was at this time that I got back in touch with a very close friend of mine, Elango, who was my senior at Titan. He had subsequently moved to the telecom sector as one of the first employees in the mobile telephony business.

After five years in Spice Telecom, he had got a job as the chief operating officer at Airtel Kerala, one of the newly acquired seven licences of Bharti Telecom. He put me on to the people at Airtel, and, by next week, I had a new job: General Manager Sales at Airtel Tamil Nadu.

It was difficult leaving Mumbai for a small town like Coimbatore. It also meant Jayu would have to leave her job at Vodafone (then Hutchison Telecom) Mumbai and take a break from work. But after careful consideration, we decided that it would be the best thing to do. We had two kids by then, Ananya and Advay. It would be good for Jayu to take a break and spend time with the kids. Moreover, telecom was a sunrise industry, and becoming the sales GM of a telecom circle was a big thing.

So we moved to Coimbatore and Airtel Tamil Nadu in 2001. I was thirty-three at that time. I did not know it then, but I was just preparing for a deep dive into the fire from the comfort of the frying pan.

I learned two things...

1. It is not very hard to acquire industry-specific knowledge. A far more important criterion for a good employee is the willingness to learn and handle tough situations.
2. A ten-fold salary hike need not get you happiness.

12. Career Leap

Airtel Tamil Nadu was headquartered in the beautiful small city of Coimbatore (the second largest city in the state and the cleanest by far) with a population of 1.3 million. The overall territory of the circle (the territory covered by the licence) spanned the entire state except capital Chennai, as also the Union territory of Pondicherry.

The telecom sector was at that point a slow-growing, loss-making sector. The whole country was divided into twenty-three circles (each state mostly comprising one circle), and two service providers were given the licence to operate in each circle. Airtel had originally bid for and acquired two licences and had then acquired another three inorganically. After about five years, the government had issued another two licences in each circle. One of them went to the state-owned Bharat Sanchar Nigam Limited (BSNL), the corporatized arm of the department of telecommunication. The other was open to existing players. Bharti Telecom, the company which owns the Airtel brand, bid and acquired seven new licences. Tamil Nadu and Kerala were the two in south India.

Telecom operations are very highly capital intensive

and extremely high in terms of operational complexity. Because of this, the head of a telecom circle is a very senior role. Many of the circle heads were CEOs or managing directors of other companies who had moved into telecom. The sales head, with the largest team reporting to him, was the No. 2 in the circle.

When I joined, I was among the first few employees in the circle, and we were operating out of one large rented room, some 1,500 sq. ft in area. There were tables and chairs strewn around the place, and it was a completely open office, with even the COO—the circle head—sitting at a table next to all of us.

The next few months were an interesting and exciting time for me. The COO, SV, was one of the most knowledgeable persons in the industry. He had been the chief financial officer (CFO) of the Chennai circle and was a seasoned telecom employee who had seen many ups and downs in that operation. His favourite statement to all of us was: 'You are allowed to do everything that is not expressly prohibited'. I gained a lot of knowledge from him regarding telecom operations. At the same time, as far as sales operations were concerned, he completely left me alone to take my own decisions.

This is where my Compaq and 3Com experience really helped. I was used to being thrown into the middle of the ocean, learning to swim and then reaching the shore.

In the next few months, I went into an overdrive—recruiting a team almost from scratch, identifying potential distributors for the prepaid business, identifying potential franchisees for the postpaid business, identifying franchisee retail locations, empanelling architects to give a standard look to the showrooms, creating the terms of trade from scratch, mapping competition, and so on. It was exhilarating work.

The entire sales infrastructure was ready well in advance of the network being set up. In fact, too much in advance.

As an organization, we had underestimated the complexity of erecting and commissioning 200-odd base transceiver stations (BTS) across the state. The launch kept getting delayed.

Moreover, we set a really aggressive target for ourselves: that of achieving 1,00,000 customers in three months. At that time, the two competitors, Aircel and BPL, had 1,80,000 and 1,30,000 subscribers respectively, whom they had acquired in about four years. So our target was insane to say the least.

In the pre-launch period, franchisees were deployed to get orders. Each of them had sales teams of ten to twelve people moving around their respective territories, getting the Intent-To-Purchase from potential subscribers. Unfortunately, no order could be closed, because we did not have the final tariffs in place; these were to be revealed closer to the launch so as not to alert the competition. As the launch kept getting delayed, the cash burn of the franchisees kept increasing. Month after month, they pumped money into the business without any returns. But my team kept their spirits up. After all, if the circle were to achieve 1,00,000 customers in three months, all the franchisees would have accomplished such a high volume of sales that they would be swimming in commission.

We were very confident of ourselves. We had a great team, a national brand, deep pockets and, above all, a new technology—untested in India—called 1800 MHz spectrum. All the other operators were using another technology: 900MHz. We told our partners and potential customers that our technology would be far superior to that of our competition and that voice clarity on our network would be far better.

Finally, the D-Day was upon us. Sunil Bharti Mittal, the group CEO and chairman, was at the launch. We were on a high.

But in the first month, we managed only 3,000 connections! When it came to actually paying the money and ordering the connections, many from the long list of prospective customers, who had evinced interest in signing up, backed out. We had made the fatal error of not testing our prospect base rigorously before projecting. Then we suffered another big blow. The 1800 MHz technology proved to have one fatal drawback: the radius of the range of an 1800MHz BTS was about half of that of a 900 MHz BTS. This meant our customers did get far better voice clarity, provided they could actually get the network to be able to talk—which was a rare and happy occasion!

The few subscribers we had started cancelling their connections or, in the case of prepaid ones, switching over to competition. This was when we compounded our mistakes. Out of desperation to achieve the 1,00,000 subscriber figure, we went berserk. We dropped the activation fee and initial deposit for new connections to zero. I, as the head of sales, should have thought through the consequences. My only excuse is that I was new to the industry.

The franchisees, now desperate to start earning commission, loosened the process. The salesmen of the franchisees went wild. They started collecting databases of people, filling up fictitious application forms and activating new mobile connections for fictitious customers.

The activation numbers went through the roof. At first, we were thrilled. We convinced ourselves that these were all genuine new customers queuing up for our connections.

In actuality, we were building an atom bomb right under our butts—and feeling damn proud about it too. The head of our postpaid sales team recognized the danger first and called me up. We put a complete stop to the scheme of zero entry cost for connections.

The atom bomb exploded when we started sending out monthly bills to all these 'customers'. We started getting calls from irate customers, mostly people of standing who said we had sent them bills even though they had never asked for connections.

In the next couple of months, multiple piles of shit started hitting multiple fans; it was fecoventilatory collision of the worst kind.

1. We decided not to pay commission to the franchisees for connections which were not being used; most of their revenues got wiped out.

2. Franchisees, in turn, started taking back commissions they had paid to sales executives, leading to huge attrition of franchisee staff.

3. The number of complaints from agitated 'customers', who were getting calls for unused connections, went through the roof.

4. We were booking revenues by way of monthly rent from fictitious customers, and this false revenue was building up.

5. We were reporting a subscriber base that did not exist.

A lot of these problems were not attributable to me or the sales team. There were processes such as customer verification, deactivation of fictitious connections, etc. which should have been followed. However, the responsibility for bringing in these connections lay completely with the sales team and, hence, squarely me.

This was a big learning for me. I learned that whatever function one handles, one has to look at the larger picture and ensure one's function contributes to achieving the larger goal.

All the issues highlighted above led to an even bigger problem—the mother of all messes. Most of the franchisees had become bankrupt by then. They had invested in showroom interiors and salaries for three to four months of the pre-launch period. And now their commissions were being taken back because their sales executives had falsified documents.

What started as murmurs from individual franchisees slowly took the form of a collective complaint. The one thing that every sales channel manager is mortally scared of is this: channel partners (franchisees, distributors, dealers, etc.) ganging up against him. And it had turned to reality. I had to diffuse the situation. I decided to take the bull by the horns. I called thirty-odd franchisees for a meeting. I was extremely apprehensive about the outcome but pushed myself to face the situation head-on.

I will never forget that day. It was a large round-table meeting. Even though there were some five team members accompanying me, I was really alone for all practical purposes. Facing me were about thirty franchisees, every one of whom wanted to beat me up for leading him up the garden path. The first hour was for them to vent their pent-up fury. I patiently listened. It was important for them to blow off steam.

Then I spoke. I owned up to the mistakes that we— Airtel—had made. I spoke of our original plans and how the deviations had occurred. I summarized the situation and where we all stood. Then I spoke of our plans going forward—deploying additional BTSes, how many in each town and how we planned to take inputs from them to understand the holes in the coverage. I spoke of the long term and how the situation would turn around.

The meeting lasted several hours, but we all left the meeting as friends, with specific action points which could help each of us. The situation was diffused.

At the end of the year, there was a decision by Airtel's top management to merge the two circles of Tamil Nadu and Chennai into one unified operation. The position of

Tamil Nadu COO was done away with, and all functional heads of the TN circle started reporting directly to more senior people in Chennai who were responsible for the combined operation.

The team members of the TN circle were completely demoralized. To them, it looked like a scaling down of operations in TN. I was the seniormost person left there. I could see that although the other functions had seasoned and excellent bosses in Chennai, they all needed some level of local support from a senior person.

I had two options: to focus on sales and marketing and do a really good job and coordinate with the other functional heads in Chennai for their deliverables OR I could take on the leadership of the circle.

I chose the second. I was available for anyone irrespective of function or role to ask support from. I had also learned a huge lesson from my earlier mistakes: one should always think of the end-to-end impact of one's and one's department's actions. I was now a changed man, to the extent that even at the cost of sales numbers, I would stick to what was overall right for the circle and for the sustainable growth of the business.

We were also lucky to get an allocation of a large capital expense budget. This meant we could set up new BTSes and improve coverage. SV had really fought for this when he was the COO, and I was reaping the benefit. We deployed everyone in the circle to improve network by identifying gaps, helping acquire space for constructing towers, giving constant feedback to the technical department, etc.

I used another weapon which I had come to be familiar with from my 3Com days: PR. I set myself a target of at least two press releases every month, and the story was again and again the same—new BTSes coming from Airtel.

Luckily for me, my new boss, P. Swaminathan, the CEO for the South India hub, was an amazing teacher. He was every bit as aggressive and given to taking risks as Ravi Swaminathan. If you take Ravi, remove the porcupine and add a professor, you might get P. Swaminathan. He was obsessed with business excellence and understood the importance of processes very well. Under his constant tutelage (and at times not delivered very politely!), I finally learned the meaning of the term 'General Manager'. Where Ravi Swaminathan had taught me the meaning of end-to-end ownership, P. Swaminathan stepped in and taught me how to apply that in a complete business scenario. Slowly, inch by inch, he helped transform my focus from gross activations of new connections to net activations (new connections minus customers who leave us), to revenue, to bottom line and to sustainable growth. It was a huge transformation. The next year was a continuous uphill struggle and we took a lot of beating against our target. But Swami stood behind me like a rock. He took on all the pressure from head office on his own shoulders, at the same time encouraging and supporting me continuously.

Manoj Kohli, the president of Airtel Mobility, was another huge supporter. He was aware of the pressure we were under and visited us multiple times to motivate the team.

Raghu, my actual functional boss, vice president, sales and marketing, south India, was completely understanding and supportive. Not only did he not stand in the way even once but he also took a lot of the load of sales planning off me and gave me time to focus on other business aspects. He never ever felt insecure. True leaders help their subordinates grow and never feel insecure about it.

At the end of that year, I was made the Circle Head for TN. At thirty-five, I was one of the youngest ever independent circle heads in the telecom industry in the country. I was the right person in the right place at the right time. My franchisees gave me a nice nickname for having managed all the channel issues adroitly and for keeping the franchisees under firm control: Ring Master. For the last two quarters of that year, Airtel TN became the leader in revenue growth and customer satisfaction in the circle.

I thought I had arrived in life. Of course, fate was gleefully rubbing its hands and muttering, 'Ha! Just you wait, you punk!'

I learned many things…

1. In a job, it is extremely important to understand the big picture and work with that in mind.
2. Never restrict your role to your job definition. Those who succeed in a job are those who take on more than expected of them.
3. Never brush problems under the carpet. Face them head-on.
4. Do the thing you fear most and the death of fear is certain.
5. Ensure you get at least one Swaminathan as a boss in your lifetime.

13. Double Whammy

I was moved to a more independent role as COO of Kerala in 2005, reporting to the executive director of the entire South India operations.

Kerala, under Elango, was one of the most successful operations in the country among the new circles in terms of revenue and profitability. It was the only profitable 1800 MHz circle in all of India. It had hit upon a gold mine in terms of revenue: Gulf calling. My knowledgeable reader would know that many countries in the Middle East are an extension of Kerala—the United Arab Emirates, Qatar, Oman and Saudi Arabia have massive Malayali populations running their economies. There was a huge quantum of international telephony that connected the migrant population with their families back home. Airtel Kerala had figured out a way of reversing the call pattern by offering a very cheap rate to some telephone booth operators in north Kerala. They would use their Airtel phones to call the migrant in the Gulf country and then put him in touch with his family members in their house in Kerala. Thirty per cent of the revenue from the circle came from this segment. A month after I took over, government regulations regarding international telephony changed and Gulf calling became completely unviable as a business.

So the circle's monthly revenue plummeted 30 per cent, and I was left holding the baby. What was worse, the next year's targets were already set and agreed to, assuming a stiff month-by-month revenue growth from the previous base.

What followed was the most challenging year in my professional life. I had to find other ways and means of getting the revenue up, fight with head office to get the targets changed, ensure that the levels of employee satisfaction did not sag (the Kerala circle had the lowest employee satisfaction scores by far), handle a unionization of franchisees and distributors and fight numerous legal battles against PILs being filed by an activist public against us, claiming cellular radiation was detrimental to health.

In a nutshell, Airtel Kerala was as tough as a rhino's backside.

But it was not this business complexity that was my biggest worry. It was the fact that I was beginning to develop some strange symptoms.

They were niggling discomforts to start with and nothing serious; my hand would tremble a bit when I held anything, for example, a spoon or a plate; and I would feel a lack of balance every time I tried to climb down stairs.

These symptoms had actually started around the time I joined Airtel. I had even consulted a doctor who did some basic check-ups and told me I was okay. I jokingly called it my 'handshaking problem' and told everyone that we sales guys were so good at shaking hands that it was not surprising that a super sales guy like me would have a handshaking problem.

In Kerala, the problem started becoming a lot more serious. My fingers, which had been progressively shaking more and more, now started showing visible signs of weakening and lack of flexibility. I also started finding it very difficult to balance myself while climbing steps. My legs felt shaky and weak.

I decided to attack the problem head-on. I put myself on an intense regimen of daily gym workouts. But by the end of each session, my hands and legs would be trembling uncontrollably.

There were just four steps leading up to my office, but I started feeling scared of climbing even those. What if I fell? I started asking my driver to carry my laptop bag— something a lot of senior execs would do but a practice I had found very snooty. Now, carrying the bag made me even more unstable.

Being the head of a telecom operation was quite a big thing in a medium-sized town like Kochi. I would be called as a chief guest for various events. Unfortunately, I knew this would entail climbing up to the podium on makeshift wooden steps—an extremely stressful and difficult task for me. I started declining most of these invitations.

I was invited as the chief guest to the Kochi Navy Ball in 2006 along with Vice Admiral S.C.S. Bangara, the No. 2

person in the navy. This was a high-profile event, and it was telecast on TV. I was one of the judges of the Navy Queen event, which was the high point of the ball. Through the whole event, instead of enjoying the beauty of the participants I was sitting with, I had a cold clammy feeling in the pit of my stomach. I was worried how I would manage to climb the four steps to the podium to crown the Navy Queen. The relief I felt when I managed to get through the sequence of events successfully and safely was immense.

Another visit to the doctor was again without a diagnosis. We were worried. What if the problem became much worse and I could not work? Jayu had quit her job when we moved to Coimbatore. Now it looked imperative that she find herself a job. But Kochi had no big companies headquartered there, and the only senior HR roles available for her would have been in other telecom companies. We decided that she should get a job in Bangalore and move there. Then, over time, the kids and I would move.

She got a couple of meaty offers in Bangalore, but then when it came to actually taking them up, we chickened out. Making the kids stay away from either of the parents was not something worth doing.

It was at this time that I was offered a role in Dell Computers. (I had been offered the same role a year previously and had declined it after Airtel's top management, including Sunil Mittal, spoke to me and persuaded me to stay.) The job was in Hyderabad as Director Sales for England and Ireland. Dell did all its consumer sales online or through call centres, and the Hyderabad team handled all the sales for England and Ireland from the call centre there. There was a person from Europe who was handling the role at the time. I was to work with him on the role as a shared responsibility (Dell called it 'two-in-a-box') for a year, and then he would go back to Germany, with me solely in charge. Though it was not a general managerial role like the one I was handling at Airtel, it was a big job, with a team of close to 800 people and handling revenue of close to a billion dollars.

I decided to move so that Jayu could find a job in the bigger city.

I learned two things...

1. Achieving a difficult professional milestone at a young age is not the end-all of everything. You need balance in life.
2. Working in Kerala is a bit like a combination of having high voltage applied to you and being bludgeoned in the back of the neck intermittently. There's no dearth of excitement.

14. Gimme a Damn Job

During my stint in Airtel, I had grown tremendously as a professional. From a mere manager, I had grown to become a manager of managers who managed managers. I had also learned how to handle huge complexity of operations and how to take end-to-end business ownership. I had learnt a lot. Airtel was an extraordinarily well-run company with a leader we all looked up to. It was difficult moving out of Airtel and the telecom sector after five years. It was even more difficult giving up a high-profile and challenging role, and leaving people I had admired and enjoyed working with, like Swami, Elango and Raghu.

The only saving grace was that I was moving to a role which was big and I would have a huge span in terms of subordinates. Dell was also known to be a great company to work in. Most importantly, in a large city like Hyderabad, Jayu would be able to find a job commensurate with her experience and education.

Consequently, I landed up in Hyderabad at the Dell office with a lot of anticipation and full of beans.

In the first couple of days, there were a series of meetings fixed for me with other directors and senior people in the

Hyderabad office. I loved the overall atmosphere of the call centre. It was full of life, with the average age of the workforce being just twenty-six. It was like being on campus all over again—though with one very important difference. Dell was extremely strict about its policy regarding the use of expletives in office. So my repertoire of 'highly impactful words', which I knew in about ten Indian languages and about half a dozen foreign languages, was completely useless. If I had to express myself freely, the only option available was making faces.

The feeling of sheer joy I experienced in the first couple of days at Dell slowly started waning. The reason? My boss, the site director for Hyderabad, dragged his feet on sending out a communication regarding my arrival to the team. Without that, at every interaction, I had to first explain who I was and what I was doing. Worse, I began to sense an undercurrent of unease among the people who were to be my direct reports.

After waiting patiently for a couple of days, I started pushing Jaideep, the site director, for action. I was baffled when he kept dodging this. They were a terribly uncomfortable couple of weeks.

That was when Jaideep suggested that the head of consumer business for the European markets wanted me to first do a few projects and understand the overall business scenario and get to know all the internal stakeholders for a few months and then take up my role. I readily agreed, but this only confirmed my feeling that there was something Jaideep was not telling me.

What seemed to have happened was that Mark, who was handling the role, had convinced his dotted-line bosses in Europe that the two-in-a-box was a bad idea and I was not required. Jaideep, in the meanwhile, had offered me the job. But the dotted-line bosses in Europe had prevailed, and by the time I landed in Dell, they decided to do away with my role. Hence, I was without a job.

I felt like a beauty queen preening herself in front of an admiring crowd just before someone comes and viciously boots her: startled, let down, amazed, shocked and ashamed to show my face.

But Jaideep, a great people manager, was working behind the scenes to get me a more meaningful role. So one day he called me over and asked me, 'RamG, we have been trying to create a certification programme for assessing agent capability. Romi (Jaideep's boss and the managing director of Dell's Indian operations) is looking for someone to lead that. Are you interested?'

Creating a certification was pure HR work. Even though I had HR heads reporting to me in my earlier role, I really did not have the HR understanding required to pull that off. Creating a certification of Dell's call taking agents also required knowledge of Dell processes, understanding of technical troubleshooting, familiarity of Dell products, etc. My score was zero on all counts. The role was that of an individual contributor, with no one reporting to me. I had just come here from a role where I could lord it over a circle of 300-odd people, having managers of managers of people managers reporting to me, with a comprehensive

profit-and-loss responsibility, handling a revenue of
Rs 300 crore and an annual investment of over Rs 400 crore.
I had been promised a billion-dollar revenue and a team
size of 800. Now I was to be an individual contributor
making a certification!

I said yes.

For me, every one of the negatives that I so dramatically
laid out in the previous paragraph looked like an interesting
challenge. This was an opportunity to learn the process of
every Dell call centre operation. It was an opportunity to
meet leaders of all different businesses. It was an opportunity
to learn all about creating a certification (something I had
no clue whatsoever about). In a nutshell, it was a learning
opportunity of a lifetime. Nothing turns me on more than
a learning opportunity, with the exception perhaps of
Angelina Jolie.

I must once again thank my father for this positive
attitude. As a chief engineer in the Kerala State Electricity
Board, he had delivered some massive projects well ahead
of schedule. Finally, he had been entrusted with a World
Bank–funded project worth several billion dollars. Since
he was impeccably honest, some vested interests managed
to have him removed from that post. He was shunted to
the role of chief engineer, human resources, a role largely
seen as parking ground for inefficient officers before
retirement. However, he had jumped into the role with so
much zeal and zest that he transformed it into a vibrant,
high-energy function which positively touched every part
of the organization. From him, I had learned that the only

question one should ask in a role is how much value one can add to it.

Jaideep offered me the new role that evening. Next morning, I was up at five, taking the first flight to Bangalore. That day, I met close to fifteen people. I worked till 3 a.m., well into the wee hours of the next morning. Dell centres in India were 24x7 operations, and we handled back-end processes or calls from Australia, EMEA (Europe, Middle East and Africa), Canada and USA. So it was not difficult to go all the way till 3 a.m. and meet all relevant people.

By the time I hit the bed that morning, I knew what a competency framework is; I broadly knew what the competencies that needed to be measured for the certification were; and I knew what the different stakeholders—HR, recruitment, training, tech support management, sales management, customer care management, agents, and so on—wanted from the certification. I also had a rough idea of who all in India, the UK and Round Rock (Dell headquarters) would be the interested parties.

In the next couple of weeks, I met up with people in each business and managed to excite a lot of them regarding the initiative.

Around this time, there was a cross-functional meeting of representatives of various functions and geographies in Round Rock to discuss the overall agent capability initiatives. I was sent as the India representative.

I went and presented a plan as per which the Indian

team would launch its own certification in three months. There were general murmurs of consternation around the room from the thirty-odd people from across geographies and functions. It was obvious that they did not want India to do its own thing without aligning with the rest of the world.

The next three days were extraordinarily interesting. I continuously pushed myself outside my comfort zone, asking for meetings with various senior people at Round Rock and taking them through my plans and seeking their support. I also realized that there was a larger agent certification initiative that was being planned at the head office. It might take longer for a global initiative to take shape, but it would have everyone's support. I also realized that if the HQ put its might behind it, the budgets that could get allocated, and hence the quality of the final output, would be of the next level. So I merged the India initiative with the global plan and became an active member of the global agent certification project.

The next year was one of tremendous learning for me. I learned how to function and at times lead in a global scenario. I learned cross-cultural etiquette and cultural sensitivities. I learned programme management from the masters of the art: the Americans. I learned how to build strong professional relations across the globe by being responsible, taking ownership and pushing the envelope in terms of my job definition. As I became an integral and respected core member of this high-profile global initiative, my positioning in the India team also grew. Jaideep pushed a lot of interesting initiatives my way. I was part of several initiatives in the India call centre space for Dell. I always took on more than what was expected of me. I was rewarded with respect and appreciation by the leadership team in India.

I also managed to make some extremely good friends in the US, people for whom I have deep respect because of their professionalism.

The high point was when I got on the stage with Romi and Michael Dell and inaugurated the global certification programme.

I learned two things...

1. The boundaries of your job are limited only by your imagination.
2. Americans are not loathsome capitalist pigs. If one opens one's mind, one can learn hugely from their culture, their professionalism and their inclusiveness.

15. Diagnosis

As soon as we shifted to Hyderabad, an incident took place which affected me deeply. The four of us—the two kids, Jayu and I—had sat down to play carom one evening. When my turn came to strike, I realized that my fingers did not have the strength required to push the striker. Try as I might, it would only move about a couple of inches.

My son, Advay, who was just six at that time, looked on in wonder as I tried again and again to generate some force. 'Acham (which is what my kids call me lovingly) can't move the striker!' he said, completely surprised that this big adult in his life could not even perform a simple task like flicking the striker.

I quickly made a joke about the situation by using my whole hand to shoot the striker and make the kids laugh. I was good at clowning around and making them laugh uproariously. But I could see that my wife was terribly worried.

Jayu could not be faulted for being worried, since the symptoms I showed were almost exactly the same as the ones her mother had: difficulty of fine motor movements, poor balance, weakening of muscles, etc. Her mother had passed away within five years of her symptoms starting. In fact, Jayu was even scared of consulting a doctor. What if he were to make the dreaded diagnosis: Motor Neuron Disease (MND)?

But my attitude was exactly the opposite. If I had MND, I wanted to know immediately. I had learned that one should never brush problems under the carpet; one should face them head-on. So we made an appointment with a senior doctor in a good hospital and went there. Since my sister-in-law, a senior functionary in the income tax department, had put in a word, we got royal treatment. The doctor conducted all possible tests; some of them involved passing currents through my peripheral nerves and measuring the conduction speed. There was a particularly painful one which involved piercing a needle deep into the muscle and then straining the muscle.

After the entire battery of tests, the doctor gave his verdict. The good news: it was not MND. The bad news: it was Charcot–Marie–Tooth disease, which is genetic and incurable. His word of consolation was that my trajectory seemed slow, and I would not have to make too many lifestyle adjustments (for example, being in a wheelchair, etc.) in the near future.

My wife and her sister were relieved beyond belief. I was not. I wanted a cure.

I adopted a multi-pronged strategy. I got back to daily walks of about forty-five minutes, and I started to attend yoga sessions every alternate day. If modern medicine had no cure, I was determined to find it somewhere.

I also contacted an Ayurvedic doctor and went for some sessions of traditional oil massages.

Initially, these strategies seemed to be working. My balance improved somewhat, and I could feel my walking speed increase marginally. The real challenge came when I had to travel to the US. Jetlag increased the trembling of my fingers. Climbing into the bathtub in hotels was even scarier. I was extremely prone to slipping and falling, and I had to stand carefully by holding onto the tap with one hand while completing my bath with minimal movements.

The initial improvement that the yoga lessons brought about started waning after some time, and my condition started deteriorating again. I decided to get admitted to an Ayurvedic hospital for a full course. There was a branch of the Coimbatore Arya Vaidyashala in Hyderabad. It was about an hour away from home, and I decided to get admitted there for a three-week treatment. It included multiple oil massages, yoga, strict diet, etc.

Since Jayu had started working in Google, she and the kids could visit me only over the weekends. I was quite lonely. On the morning of the second day, I went for a yoga session and the instructor told me to follow what the others were doing at my own pace. But being one to always push the boundaries, I tried my level best to match them. The pace was intense, and I kept up.

But I had to pay a huge price for my over-enthusiasm. The effect of the Ayurveda treatment, combined with the intense over-exertion, was disastrous. By that evening, I could not lift my arms. However hard I tried, my arms refused to go above shoulder level. They would also tremble uncontrollably every time I tried to pick up anything. My fingers were so weak and insensate that they became almost completely useless. When dinner was served in the room (a plate of rice, sabzi and a couple of chapatis), it took me over an hour to finish the food, because I could not hold the spoon in my hand.

I did not want to worry Jayu and kept all this from her.

One night, I had a visitor. I woke up on hearing a soft thudding sound that repeated every thirty seconds or so. I reached out for the switchboard and put on the light, looking around to figure out what had caused the sound. I could see nothing. I put off the light. After about fifteen minutes, just when I was drifting back to sleep, the sound started again. I put on the light again and looked around. This time I saw it: a little mouse scurrying under the bed to hide from the light.

I was petrified. I had serious issues with anything furry and squishy. And here were furriness and squishiness in their grossest form hiding under my bed. There was one more problem. I was now scared of getting out of bed. In case the mouse ran out at that time, I knew I would involuntarily jerk my feet or try to jump. In my case, this would mean a certainty of falling down and breaking something. The only option was to keep the lights on and hope the mouse would go away.

But then, the mouse had to find a way out. As I sat up and watched, I realized what the soft thud sound was. The mouse had entered the room through a small hole in the ceiling and had used the curtains to climb down. Having figured out that the room was not the best place for it, it was trying to climb back up the curtains and then jump from the pelmet to the hole it had come through. The hole was too far up, and it kept falling to the floor with a soft thud. It kept repeating the process with monotonous regularity.

It was obvious that doing the same thing again and again was not going to get the mouse the desired result even after a hundred attempts. But it still kept at it. (Unlike what happened with King Robert the Bruce and the spider, there was no life lesson for me to learn from this mouse. Stupid mouse ☺.)

The next day was terrible for me. Not only was I unable to use my hands properly but, added to that, I had also had a totally sleepless night.

That was when I made the mistake of Googling my condition. The doctor had warned me that CMT was incurable and irreversible, and so I had not done too much of research on it. Now I saw just how terrible the condition was and just how bad it could get. The images of CMT patients available online were graphic and very, very scary.

I wanted so much to speak to someone and unburden myself. I could not call Jayu and worry her. The only person I could think of was my father. He was strong as steel and could always be counted on.

I called him and told him about the condition and how it was irreversible and how much worse it could get over time. As I spoke to him, the helpless and hopeless feeling that had built up over the past couple of days burst like a dam. I cried my heart out over the phone. That was one of the lowest points in my life. I am sure my father's heart must have broken with grief. But he was stoic, sympathetic and encouraging.

I felt enormously lighter and better after that. I also told myself that come what may, I would not give up hope. I would try every possible means to cure myself; and if modern medicine did not work, I would try Ayurveda; if that did not work, I would try Reiki, naturopathy, karmic healing—whatever it took.

I completed the course, but it did not improve the condition much. The doctor gave me a bit of strong advice when I was discharged. He felt that working at night (from 5 p.m. to 3 a.m. in those days) was detrimental to my condition; proper sleep was essential.

It was at this juncture that I was made an offer to join Hewlett Packard (HP) as director, operations. Ravi Swaminathan, my former boss at Compaq, was now president of one division of HP India and thought that I could add a lot of value in HP, and it was his recommendation that set the ball rolling. It felt great to be headhunted by an old boss.

Joining HP would mean moving to Delhi, but it also meant not having to work late nights in a call centre operation. Jayu could get a transfer to Google Delhi. Also, the role was big. I would be reporting to the head of volume operations in Asia Pacific, with a dotted-line link to Ravi.

I accepted the offer, and we moved to Gurgaon in 2008. I was forty.

I learned two things...

1. Being brave does not mean having no fear. It is the ability to smile and handle the situation with a calm mind even while one's heart is quaking within oneself.
2. Don't look for life lessons in every random act of stupidity performed by animals and insects.

16. From the Frying Pan...

HP was the No. 1 computer hardware company in the world. It had acquired Compaq a few years previously, which was the reason Ravi Swaminathan was now in HP. It also had many of my ex-colleagues from my Compaq days.

But the similarity ended there. Compaq used to be a highly leveraged, efficiently run, fast-paced organization. HP was an incredibly huge and bureaucratic behemoth of an organization. Like most US companies, it had a matrix structure. Indian business was handled by three presidents (based on product lines) who reported to their individual Asia Pacific bosses. Ravi was one of the three. There were functions like mine—operations, finance, HR—which supported all the three business groups but whose heads reported to their respective Asia Pacific (APAC) heads. Since my predominant internal customer was Ravi's team, I also had a dotted-line reporting to him. The structure was great. The products were fantastic. But the sheer size of the organization made coordination and collaboration a huge challenge.

Since all complex business issues required all functions

to work together, it was imperative that someone took end-to-end responsibility for each problem. We also had a huge and complex task on our hands. A big chunk of HP's business came from the government. Collecting cash from the government for products sold was an extraordinarily difficult task. This meant that HP had a large outstanding amount in its books.

For me, coming from the end-to-end model of Airtel, these glaring issues were unbearable. I dived into them with gusto.

I was warned by many well-wishers that it was important to first ensure that every decision I took was approved by all and to never take any risky decision, even if it meant losing business. There were rumours making the rounds about people who were sacked for not playing it safe. But then, my belief was absolutely to the contrary: people like me were there to take risks.

There were many people who told me that it would be wiser for me to internally fight for stopping the government business, since handling the operations for this part of the business was highly risky. I found this attitude difficult to digest. Leaders in organizations are supposed to handle tough problems, not hide from them. If I ran away from this, I would come down in my own estimation. I supported the government business completely and started working towards ensuring that all safeguards were in place so that we or our partners did not fault on ethical compliance.

I also realized that the company was bleeding due to large overdue payments from customers across the board.

Due to cost optimization, collections were being handled by a central hub in Malaysia. Since Indian customers were much more used to a personalized touch from their vendors, the collection team found it difficult to get money out of many customers. I, on the other hand, had a large team spread across the country. I spoke to them about the importance of driving collections and urged them to get into it.

Things were going well when life took a huge turn for the better and for the worse.

About four months into the job, my uncle, Dr Balakrishnan, a renowned doctor in Kerala, fixed up a comprehensive check-up for me with the head of neurology in his hospital. After three days of tests, the doctor made his diagnosis. My condition was not CMT. It was an autoimmune disorder called Chronic Inflammatory Demyelinating Polyneuropathy (CIDP). My own immune system was mistakenly identifying the nerves in my arms and legs as pathogens and was attacking them. This was destroying the sheath around the nerves called myelin. Without myelin, the nerves could not transmit impulses to the muscles, making it difficult for me to move these limbs. Over time, unused muscles were also atrophying. Fortunately, the condition had some known treatments to reverse it. A cousin, Hari, a highly qualified neurologist from the US, also examined me (luckily he was in Kerala at that time) and came to the same conclusion. Just to make sure there was no mistake in the diagnosis, the doctor took a biopsy of my nerve and sent it for analysis. The result was expected in a couple of weeks.

I went back to Gurgaon to wait for the result, a new ray of hope in my heart.

But fate, I have often noticed, does not give a damn whether you are hopeful or not. It has independent plans which it executes without consulting anyone.

Which is why as soon as I got back to Gurgaon, fate threw a viral fever at me. The fever, which started as a normal mild fever, had a disastrous effect on my body. Within two days, I felt my condition spike. Over the next three days, the condition worsened to alarming proportions. I found it difficult to sit up; I couldn't move my left hand; I could barely move my right hand; I had no articulation of my left ankle (it flopped down); my left eyelid drooped (I could not keep it open); my voice became a hoarse whisper.

Jayu and Appa (who stayed with us) were at their wits' end. Jayu called up my uncle in Kochi, who in turn spoke to Dr Anathkumar—the doctor who had diagnosed the condition. He was kind enough to speak to a friend in a Delhi hospital, who in turn spoke to a neurologist in his hospital—Dr Monika Thomas. She was an extremely busy doctor but called up my wife at 10 p.m. after she reached her home in Gurgaon. After hearing my wife out patiently, at 10.30 p.m., she drove all the way to my house. She was an angel.

Within five minutes, she confirmed the diagnosis. It was CIDP, and the spike had happened because of the enhanced activity of the immune system due to the fever. She called up a local hospital, found out that the neurologist, Dr Praveen Gupta, was still on duty and requested him to wait in the hospital. She and her driver managed to get me into a chair (luckily with wheels), wheeled me into her car, took me to the hospital, met Dr Gupta, explained her diagnosis, recommended the treatment and then left at midnight.

There are many, many people to whom I am grateful for the kindness they have shown to me. Dr Monika will always be right at the top.

The treatment I was put on was a full course of IVIG (Intravenous Immuno-Globulin). About thirty-two bottles of IVIG had to be intravenously administered over five days. It was a thick liquid, and a single vein could not handle so much of the liquid. Over those five days, I was poked and the vein changed half a dozen times. The treatment cost Rs 6 lakh. But it was worth every paisa of it.

By the end of the fifth day, my voice came back; my eyelid stopped drooping; I could lift my hand to scratch my nose (a critical requirement, especially when one couldn't do it) and sit up. I was discharged.

What happened in the next couple of weeks was mind-blowing. I was like Asterix after a quick swig of the magic potion. One by one, body parts that were in near disuse started mending. My wrists and biceps, which were extremely weak, suddenly became stronger; my gait became normal after about five years; my voice, which had started piping over the previous year, became strong again.

I was on top of the world. I started an intense series of exercises to get back to normal as soon as possible—lifting weights, walking, doing push-ups, etc. I started climbing the eight floors to my office. I started teaching my son cricket. I went shopping with the kids. We bought all the ingredients and I made a pizza for them—something I could not have done at any time in the previous three years. We had so much fun. That month, my kids must have realized for the first time that I was not only funny while telling stories but I was also a fun guy to hang around with and full of energy—as I used to be years back.

But that was a flash in the pan. The effect of IVIG lasted only for about a month. At the end of that period, the condition returned—this time settling well below the previous baseline. I was baffled and disappointed. The doctor had not even hinted that this might happen. I had assumed that I was cured for good. I had built so many castles in the air—from running a marathon by the next year to playing cricket with my son to climbing Machu Picchu—all the things I had wanted to do but had shelved for years and which had suddenly seemed to be within arm's length.

This time the doctor put me on a smaller dose of IVIG—a fifth of the first, primarily because we could not afford Rs 6 lakh every second month. He also put me on an alternative treatment—a far less expensive one but fraught with side effects. It was a daily dose of prednisone, a steroid.

The doctor started me off on 30 mg of prednisone. Every second month, I had to get admitted to the hospital for two days for a short dose of IVIG. Each time, within a week of the dose, my condition would improve somewhat but would take a deep dive within about forty-five days.

It was while I was in hospital for one such IVIG treatment that the bombshell came. I got a call from Pat, my boss, asking me if I had checked my mail. Apparently, an email had been sent to me, her, some other senior people in the organization, a few senior people in our customer accounts, etc., alleging serious malpractices in a department which rolled up to me. The anonymous person also claimed he was no longer with HP and that the malpractice had been going on for several years. He also named two persons (managers) in my team as responsible.

Pat asked me if I knew anything about the alleged malpractice. (I cannot divulge the details since this would mean revealing confidential information.) I was totally taken aback and told her I had no idea. However, I had a reasonable hypothesis that one of the three contract employees who had been terminated the previous week must have sent the email.

Over the next several months, there was an intense internal investigation. For me, it was an extraordinarily challenging period. I had to ensure that the investigating team got all the possible support. I also had to ensure that business continued as usual without interruption. There was a massive government order which had to be executed flawlessly; there was the huge existing outstanding which had to be collected and which required many internal organizations to be pushed and prodded; and my health was deteriorating rapidly. After each IVIG infusion, the baseline would settle a bit lower than the previous time. The dosage of prednisone kept going up to try and compensate—from 30 mg per day to 40 to 50 to 60 to 80 mg per day. The side effects were disastrous.

I bloated up by 15 kg and started looking like a football; my eyesight started fading (prednisone causes a deposit to form on the cornea); I had to stop driving as my foot couldn't be trusted to press the clutch or brake properly and neither did my hands have enough strength to change the gears. These were all the massive difficulties I faced. But there were far worse ones to follow...

Out of the blue, I experienced a spiking of the condition again. This time, the effect was to once again render the left ankle limp. Every time I lifted the left leg to step forward, the forefoot would drop down and dangle uselessly. This meant I had to be extremely careful about lifting the leg a full foot off the ground whenever I walked so that I would not trip over it. Unfortunately, once, stepping out of a lift, I did exactly that. I tripped and fell. The ankle, which had already sprained half a dozen times over the previous few years, twisted horribly. I had to start using crutches.

Equally difficult was lifting any weight with my right hand. The right biceps did not have the strength to lift more than a kilo or so. Slinging my laptop bag over my shoulder each day was a nightmare.

My fingers lost strength and sensation. I had to use my thumbs to laboriously type mails. Going to the toilet was another challenge. It was extremely difficult for my insensate and trembling fingers to locate the zip. Thanks to my bloated frame, I could not see it either. There were occasions when I had to spend ten minutes in front of the urinal while my fingers tried to find the zip. It was even more difficult since the medication I was on made me urinate frequently. Imagine having to stand ten minutes in front of the urinal while your bladder is screaming at you to GO NOW! At times, I could not find the zip after the job was done. There were occasions when I became so desperate that I nearly asked another man in the toilet to help me. I could only imagine the shocked gossip it would have spawned: Gay director hits on unsuspecting urinating employee!

My balance had become terrible. I could not even climb one step without holding onto the railing. Standing on firm ground felt like standing on a soft cotton mattress. Standing even on flat floors meant swaying continuously and fighting a toppling sensation every moment. If I had to look upwards or hold something, I would lose my balance and had to grab at something to stay on my feet.

During all this, I was determined never to drop a single ball at work. I would enter every room with a cheerful and loud 'hello'. In a meeting, I would be the one to bring in the cheer with a bit of humour. I believed that being humorous kept me positive. It made those around me positive. That positivity rubbed back on me and made me even more positive and cheerful. It was what we engineers called a positive feedback loop.

I drove my team and myself to own the company's pain

points: customer dissatisfaction, doubtful debts, delivery turnaround times, revenue recognition, gross margin maximization, process streamlining, etc. I wanted my team of operations managers to become operational excellence managers. I suspect they must have thought I was a lunatic at times, but I considered it my job to make them general manager material.

I could also be effective in solving highly complex problems which required many functions to contribute. I had no ego issues in requesting a colleague in another function to do his bit a hundred times without losing my patience. The only thought in my mind was that the goal had to be achieved.

The story was the same back home. I saw myself as the energy provider. I would spend a couple of hours every day clowning around with my kids and regaling them with funny wacky stories. They gave me enormous energy. I also knew that I could never let my shoulders droop in front of them. I wanted them to learn from me that the only way to handle tough situations was to face them head-on without flinching—and to face them cheerfully.

One huge inspiration was one of my oldest and closest family friends, Rajesh. He had been diagnosed with cancer a few years back. After undergoing chemo, the doctors had declared he was in remission. Then, a couple of years later, it had come back with a bang. The only thing that could save him was bone marrow transplant. But even in that condition, whenever I spoke to him over the phone, he would be full of humour, cracking jokes about his own condition. I wanted to be like Rajesh.

Elango and family, who were our neighbours in Gurgaon, were also a great support. We went together on all holidays, which were extremely enjoyable and helped me keep feeling positive.

I also started blogging. My blogs were humorous and had a lot of followers. Blogging funny stuff kept me positive and buoyant.

I learned two things...

1. When the going gets tough, the tough get humorous.
2. Making a driver do up your top button (which you inadvertently left unbuttoned) can be quite embarrassing and liable to making him think you are making a pass at him.

17. ...into the Fire

That Monday, just before leaving for office, I felt charged up. There were a lot of things to do, lots of problems to solve. I changed my Facebook status to 'Looking forward to another fantastic week at work'. My wife, always superstitious, scolded me. She strongly believed that anyone who openly expressed joy was liable to get a kick in the backside from fate.

When the phone rang that afternoon, I had no idea that my life was about to plunge into a deep crisis—a crisis that made the desperate situation I was already in look like a saunter in the park.

It was Patricia. The call? To tell me that she was extremely sorry but the internal investigating agency had decided after nine months of investigations that it wanted me to resign. In a nutshell, I was being politely sacked.

I doubt if many people have been in a situation like that. In today's corporate world, one can be told to put in one's papers for various reasons—non-performance, sexual harassment, unethical conduct or because the organization is downsizing for profitability reasons. But this was different. I was being told to take responsibility for misconduct that had been going on in the organization for several years before I had even joined; misconduct perpetrated by a team three levels below me; misconduct that had apparently continued to happen in the first four months of my stint and was subsequently stopped thanks to the structures I had put in place.

Unfairness brings out strong responses in human beings. When the unfairness is directed at you, the response is even stronger. I was shell-shocked when I heard what she had to say. In the previous year, after the investigation had started, not for a moment had I suspected that I would be a victim. The total unfairness of the situation hit me like a blow. For a moment, I couldn't even grasp what she was saying. Then, as the enormity of what she said struck me, I felt the blood drain from my face. I politely said a few sentences and hung up.

I sat in the small conference room for five minutes, letting the news sink in. Then I called my wife. As I told her what had happened, anger and self-pity rose up inside me. I could also feel my eyes well up helplessly. Jayu was shocked and angry. She had seen me struggle with all my health problems and still give a 110 per cent to the job. 'Baby, I am coming over to pick you up,' she said.

During the ride home, she spared no effort to control her anger. She cursed the company, cursed Patricia, cursed Ravi and all the bosses. Mostly she cursed the compliance and legal departments—those faceless persons who sat in the head office and pronounced judgment on people halfway across the globe, people they had never even seen or spoken with.

But I possessed one enormous strength. In intensely high-pressure situations, I was always able to keep calm and think clearly. I pointed out to her that Patricia was just a messenger. In HP, these decisions were taken by the legal and compliance departments. Their only job was to protect the company from being exposed to any risk. And in some way, the company was protecting itself by sacking me—to show that the company had taken strong action against wrongdoing. Line managers were never involved or consulted in those decisions. Line managers did not even question these decisions for fear of being accused of working hand in glove with the employee concerned.

At home, my parents had come to visit us from Kerala. They had come to encourage me in my difficult times and to keep my spirits up. They saw our faces and instantly knew that something was terribly wrong. Jayu and I quickly explained the situation to my parents and to Appa. None of them could believe what they heard. My father was the only one who could view the situation dispassionately. In that turbulent moment, he was like a rock.

I decided to pursue a two-pronged strategy. First, to take legal advice whether I could sue HP; second, to use all my goodwill in the organization to push for a reversal of the decision.

In the next couple of days, I contacted a couple of lawyers I knew personally. The advice was not to pursue the matter legally. It would be expensive, long-drawn-out and with very low chances of any success.

Patricia came down from Singapore. She and I shared a

fantastic equation. We were more friends than colleagues. I am sure facing me and telling me the news was tough for her.

After seeing the investigation report, it was very clear to me that while there was evidence against a couple of employees in my team, there was none about any wrongdoing by me. I felt relief and anger at the same time: relief because there was no black mark on my integrity, anger because the organization had still felt the need to fire me. Patricia heard me out and asked me to send a detailed mail to the investigating team defending myself, and she promised to buy me time and try her level best to give me an easy exit with a face saver.

I had two options. One was to stop work altogether, in which case there were many loose ends that would cause a lot of trouble for HP and perhaps impact the business for a couple of quarters. The other option was to continue working in exactly the same way I had been all this while—with full sincerity and 110 per cent ownership. I chose the latter—not out of any love for HP but because I did not want to let down all those co-workers who depended on me to solve some complex problems which I was in the best position to solve. I had learned early on in my life that one's reputation was built by one's interaction with co-workers and subordinates and it was easy to destroy that in a fit of spite. I was a professional through and through, and I would exit the company as one.

I know Pat put in a lot of effort to help me, and it was decided to give me a softer landing—three months on the rolls and I would announce my own retirement citing health issues. In the next one month, I worked my heart out. Nobody in the system had a whiff of the fact that I was serving my notice. I drove my team to stretch the boundaries of our deliverables and plug as many issues as possible. When I presented the India scorecard in the quarterly Asia Pacific regional review, there was applause from everyone. We had surpassed the targets set by all our deliverables and put up the best ever performance in all key areas.

While I was holding up the team and the operations, on the personal front, I was in deep trouble. My annual hospitalization bill was about Rs 15-20 lakh. Jayu's company, Google, had a great insurance policy, but it covered only a part of the expense. Even if I had three months to look for a job, I knew there was no way I could get one. I looked visibly ill; I could barely walk; I had to use a crutch; and I couldn't even see clearly, let alone type properly. How could I even dream of getting another job?

But I also knew it was totally and completely pointless to feel depressed about all this. I had to keep a cool head and find solutions to the problem. There was absolutely no point in cursing HP or my fate and thinking of what I had lost or of the deep pile of problems I was buried under. I had to accept reality and find a solution. And I did.

I learned two things...

1. Life is not fair. Expecting life to be nice to you just because you are nice to everyone is like expecting a tiger not to eat you just because you don't eat tigers.
2. You have very little control over circumstances. But you have complete control over how you react to circumstances.

18. Solution

By the time I left HP, I had contacted a classmate from XLRI and a good friend, Ashish, who was running a small but respected company called iDiscoveri. It was building and implementing an innovative experiential school curriculum called XSEED. It was a great cause—changing the face of education in India. The company was small, and a lot of processes were not in place. Ashish wanted me to take up a part-time consulting position in the organization. This was perfect for me as I could leverage my strengths—end-to-end business understanding, risk identification, customer orientation and process orientation. I would also have enough time on my hands to focus on physiotherapy and to search for long-term solutions to my illness. I was determined to look at all the glorious opportunities this break provided.

But fate, the sadistic so-and-so, had a different plan altogether. The day after I started my engagement at iDiscoveri, I was descending the three steps outside my apartment block to get into the car when I lost my balance, fell and twisted my ankle—yes, the same damn ankle—for the millionth time. The pain was excruciating, and it swelled up like a balloon.

That evening, my wife took me to see an orthopaedic doctor. After examining the X-Ray report, the doctor pronounced the verdict. I had a fracture and needed to be in a cast.

My heart broke. Putting me in a cast was the equivalent of confining me to a bed. Using a crutch and walking while in a cast was not an option for me because of my lack of balance. I would have to give up the consulting assignment.

As the doctor went out of the room to fetch the necessary material for the cast, I looked at my wife and the unfairness and hopelessness of the situation hit me like a blow. I also felt terrible because of all that I was putting her through. How much despair I was piling on this wonderful woman who was always there for me, who looked after my smallest need without my having to even ask. In spite of myself, my eyes welled up. 'Baby, I am so sorry. Please don't give up on me,' I said.

She looked at me, amazed that I would even say something as stupid as that. Hugging me, she said, 'Of course not, baby. Are you crazy? I will never ever give up on you.'

The cast was done very badly. It cut into my shin, and I went back the next day to have the doctor redo it. He cut a small part off the top, which made it even worse. I was lucky he could not solve the problem, because I went to see another orthopaedic doctor. He looked at the X-Ray report and told me, 'It's an old, healed fracture. You don't need the cast.' He cut it off and, sure enough, within a couple of days, my ankle healed.

I completed the consulting assignment in three months, and Ashish offered me a full-time job as COO. I also had another offer—to join as a partner—from a former colleague who had floated a private equity fund. I chose the iDiscoveri role, since I thought it would be less stressful.

I was, of course, fooling myself. With my knack for pushing the boundaries of my role, I was soon neck deep in work, with a finger firmly stuck in every other pie.

In spite of the stress, I kept two things going on the personal front: daily walks and mild exercise, and an ongoing search for a solution to my health problems.

The IVIG continued to result in small spikes of improvement, my condition falling back to a lower and lower baseline each time within forty-five days. The steroid, which had proved more or less ineffective, was replaced with Azathioprine, an immunosuppressive drug. But nothing seemed to work.

That was when my online searches finally bore fruit. I came across a clinical trial being conducted at Northwestern Memorial Hospital in Chicago for a treatment called Autologous Nonmyeloablative Hematopoietic Stem Cell Transplant. I sent in an enquiry.

I got a response immediately, saying that they were looking for patients who fitted some specific criteria and who had been suffering from CIDP. I seemed to fit the bill.

I also learned that, as luck would have it, Dr Richard Burt, who was conducting this trial, was planning to visit Bangalore in a few months. I requested for a meeting, and he was gracious enough to agree to meet me one evening.

Jayu and I travelled down to Bangalore that day. We attended a talk the doctor was giving. It was amazing. For the past several years, he had been heading the division of immunotherapy at the hospital and had treated hundreds of patients with different types of autoimmune disorders. He saved the lives of people who had given up all hope in life.

After the presentation, we had dinner together. The doctor was as humble as his achievements were lofty. He was also an incredibly well-read and knowledgeable person. I felt an instant connect with him—so much so that I reeled off my life story, including my wild days on campus, Bullet beer, rum for mules, burning crosses, etc. Jayu tried kicking me under the table but that had no effect on me. After the meeting, we were convinced that I should go through the treatment. But the doctor had a doubt whether my condition was due to excessive drinking! As soon as he went back, he politely asked me to send across all my reports so that his colleague, a neurologist, could rule out that possibility. Jayu kicked me some more—verbal kicks, that is—for my bragging.

Luckily, it turned out that the condition had nothing to do with my past 'spirituality', and it indeed looked like CIDP. So we fixed a date for the treatment.

Even though there was a small risk of mortality, I was very clear that I would go for the treatment. I wanted a complete cure. My mind wanted it so much that over the previous four years, I had had at least a dozen vivid dreams in which I was sprinting. It felt so wonderful, being able to sprint like an athlete, without a care in the world. In those dreams, I would tell myself that it was not a dream this time and that I had actually been cured. Then I would wake up feeling bitterly disappointed.

So yes, I wanted a cure. The only catch was the cost. The to-and-fro airfare and the cost of the hotel stay in downtown Chicago for three months was minuscule compared to the actual cost of the treatment. We would have to spend a large percentage of our combined savings. But if it could give me my life back, it was worth it. The risk was: what if it did not cure me? The doctor had indicated that the probability of success was about 80 per cent. What if I was part of the 20 per cent? But being an incredible optimist (almost foolishly so), I completely pushed that thought aside.

We withdrew all the various savings we had and paid the advance to the hospital.

It was in those days that I realized the importance of relatives and friends. My parents, my brother, Jayu's sister, Appa—they were all wonderfully supportive. Relatives with whom I had not even been in regular touch were incredibly supportive. Friends, ex-colleagues, XLRI and IIT classmates and even schoolmates reached out and encouraged me. I realized that there was no way I could return all their kindness. But I knew that I would return the kindness—not necessarily to them, but to anyone going through a tough phase.

Rajesh had gone through with the bone marrow transplant a couple of years earlier. It had been a complete success. His attitude, his courage and the dignity with which he handled the whole situation were an inspiration to me.

Ananya was a thirteen-year-old adult by this time and Advay a ten-year-old baby. They would be left in the care of Appa for three months. My parents were also to chip in and stay with them for a while.

Jayu and I always communicated everything openly with our kids. We called them in together and explained in simple terms the treatment I was going to go through. I explained how much I wanted to get well and how I thought this would help me. Finally, I also told them that there was some risk involved but I was confident nothing would happen to me.

Finally the day came for us to leave. Both kids stayed with us till about ten o' clock. Then Advay could not stay up anymore and slept off. About an hour before we were to leave for the airport, Ananya hugged me and started crying. She was inconsolable and kept crying till we left. I felt terrible, leaving my baby in such a state.

I learned two things...

1. You may not get an opportunity to return the kindness to every individual who has been kind to you. But you can surely be kind to every individual you have an opportunity to show kindness to.
2. Bragging about one's drinking prowess to one's doctor may not be the wisest move.

19. Resurrection

Chicago was an awesome place. The fact that we had a service apartment in the heart of the Magnificent Mile at a ridiculously cheap rate of $90 per day added to the feeling of well-being.

We also rediscovered some amazing friends in Chicago: Manish and Radhika, a couple who had been my classmates, and another classmate, Shridhar, and his wife Vasudha. They took turns bringing us food, hosting us over weekends and supporting us in various ways in spite of their busy schedules. There were also cousins in the US who Skyped with us multiple times a day to keep our spirits up, especially BalC (Balchandran), with whom I discussed everything under the sun, ranging from Barack Obama to Steve Jobs and world history.

There was a battery of tests scheduled for the first three weeks, just to make sure that the condition was CIDP and also that my body could withstand the treatment.

After the initial tests, I got a call from Paula, Dr Burt's nurse, to inform me that a particular protein level was high in my blood. This could be due to multiple myeloma, a form of blood cancer. I had to go through a bone marrow biopsy to make sure that was not the case. It took an agonizing ten more days for the test to be completed and the results to come out. I did not have blood cancer.

After the tests, it was time for the stem cell harvesting. This was done by first injecting a small dose of chemo to stimulate the bone marrow and increase the production of hematopoietic stem cells—the blood stem cells that would eventually form all types of blood cells. After about a week of the chemo, I was admitted to the hospital and connected to a centrifuge. My blood was run through it for a few hours till enough stem cells were removed.

This was followed by a four-week break. Jayu and I enjoyed this period, going around Chicago and taking in as many sights as possible. Dhananjay, a friend from IIT, came down from Seattle just to drive us around Chicago. I really did have great friends.

During all this, I was determined to do something constructive. That was when the idea of writing a book took shape. I was inspired by the life of Alex, BalG's close friend, who had become a paraplegic following an accident a week before his wedding. He had become a full-fledged technology author and had written dozens of books. There was only one minor catch: my fingers were not strong enough to type. But these small inconveniences were not going to stop me. I could use both my thumbs to type out the letters, and even though I had to pause frequently because my arms lacked the strength to remain raised for more than a few minutes at a time, I managed to complete about fifty pages.

Finally, it was time for the treatment. Jayu and I checked out of the hotel and moved into the hospital. I was admitted into a sterile ward. The patients in all the other rooms on the floor were undergoing treatment for multiple myeloma or lymphoma—forms of blood cancer.

In spite of the intense treatment I was about to go through, I loved the hospital. It was like a small five-star hotel room: a lovely huge bed, an inviting couch, a small bed for Jayu, a wonderful view of the lake from the fifteenth-floor window and, to top it all, a direct view of the head office of *Playboy!*

Jokes aside, what was really outstanding was the quality of the staff there. The nurses and the assistants were warm, encouraging and extremely professional. I was again amazed by how well things ran in the US. From being a country of capitalist pigs, it had now become one of professionalism and inclusiveness. I loved this country.

The daily visitors included Dr Burt and Amy Morgan—Dr Burt's nursing practitioner, who became a great friend. In fact, we became quite close to most of the nurses there. Some of their personal stories were quite inspiring.

Even though Dr Burt had treated hundreds of patients with multiple sclerosis and lupus, the protocol for CIDP had been started more recently. I was only the twelfth patient undergoing this treatment.

The treatment itself consisted of six days of infusion of various interesting substances: chemo, ATG (a rabbit extract) and rituxan (a hamster extract).

The earlier chemo shot—the one given before the stem

cell harvest—had made my hair fall off in clumps and I had shaved my head. This time, by the third day, I became completely weak. It was the effect of the chemo. It was also because I had been off IVIG for more than two months. I started experiencing all the usual symptoms of a delayed IVIG. I could not eat on my own; I would sway dangerously while standing up to go to the bathroom; and my voice started piping. The doctor decided to give me an infusion of IVIG.

I don't know what I would have done without Jayu. She was an angel who had been sent to Earth for the express purpose of looking after me. She had to feed me breakfast, lunch and dinner because I did not have strength to pick up the spoon. I was on medication to help frequent urination, and I had to wake her up multiple times at night to take me to the bathroom. She made sure I washed my mouth with saline water every two hours (to prevent mouth ulcers, a common side effect of chemo). From Day 5 to Day 10, when I could barely eat anything, she bought Lays chips and spicy sauce and mixed them with curd rice to give me a near approximation of South Indian food. She was there for the minutest of my needs, even helping me rank the nurses in order of prettiness.

On Day 7, the stem cells were to be infused back into my body. The hospital handled this wonderfully. It offered the services of a chaplain to bless the stem cells. We were touched and happily accepted. I was handed a huge card, signed by all the nurses, and a bag of goodies consisting of a couple of pen-shaped hand sanitizers, a water bottle and a small bag. The nurses and the chaplain all came into the room and prayed for me and the reinfusion happened.

My body had been rebooted. Now, one had to wait and see if it was repaired.

By Day 9, I became neutropenic. That is, my white blood cell count went down to zero. So did the count of lymphocytes—the T-cells and B-cells (the immune cells). Now all I had to do was generate new cells that were not confused into thinking I was a pathogen instead of being their lord and master.

By Day 10, I started feeling less like squashed roadkill and more like a human being.

My willpower, long shackled inside an unresponsive body, burst forth. I started walking the corridors with a vengeance. It must have been an interesting sight. Because of the number of different medications which had to be fed into my body intravenously, the hospital had inserted a catheter through my arm into my jugular. At any point of time, I received multiple infusions: red blood cells, plasma, chemo, ATG, rituxan, antibiotics, saline, etc. All of these were hung on a stand with wheels.

I pulled the stand along with me as I walked the corridors, with Jayu holding my other hand. My target-oriented brain quickly calculated one round of the corridor as 200 metres. On the first day, I (with Jayu firmly by my side) did three rounds. The next day, I pushed it to five. By Day 16, I was zipping down the corridor (by my own standards) and doing eight to ten rounds a day, much to the surprised delight of the nurses. I was an ideal patient.

The chemo and the rat-and-rabbit infusions had another interesting effect on me. It could be that my body mistook the chemo for my old friends, Old Monk rum and Bullet beer. I was on a general high. I did a complete U-turn on the book I was writing. It had started as a serious, darkish young adult book. Now, my chemo-pickled mind was drawn to a new genre: absurd fiction.

I was always one to take myself lightly and find humour in any situation. The numerous extempore stories I told my children had always bordered on insanity. My blog posts had always been wacky and funny. So now I decided to have Oops, an evolved pumpkin from the future, as the protagonist of my book.

On Day 18, my blood counts started going up, and, on Day 19, I was discharged.

I learned two things....

1. If one keeps an open mind, one can learn and be inspired by anything and anyone.
2. Staring at the *Playboy* building for longish periods of time is not going to make their pin-ups come jumping out.

---

20. The Excel Sheet

Sridhar and Vasudha came to pick us up. They were carrying traditional South Indian food with them.

Dr Burt was such a humble and wonderful human being. He insisted on taking Jayu and me out for dinner the next day. I guess he wanted to do this because Jayu and I had treated him to dinner when he was in Bangalore. We celebrated by downing a bottle of wine between us. I also used the opportunity to understand a lot of the science behind his work.

Bidding farewell to Chicago was like saying goodbye to my second home. In a way, this was now the place of my rebirth. I was still very susceptible to all kinds of infections. I was given a bunch of prescriptions for the next one year, and I needed to wear a mask through the return journey.

It was wonderful to return home, alive, to my kids and my parents and Appa.

The day after I got home, I prepared a detailed workout plan. There were twenty-seven muscles that I needed to exercise. I wanted to push myself to the limit. I wanted to get okay. Fast.

I drew up an Excel sheet with a daily target for exercising

each of the twenty-seven muscles. I set the target for each exercise for each day for the next six months. Each week, the target would go up marginally.

Then I set about surpassing the target each day.

Some of the worst-affected muscles were my left wrist and my right bicep. At first, I had difficulty lifting a 100 gm bottle with my left hand, holding the arm steady and just articulating the wrist. Over time, I pushed it to 200 gm, half a kg, 1 kg, 2 kg and 3 kg. Similarly, I could only lift 100 gm with my right bicep. Again over the first few months, I took this up to 3 kg.

Initially I could do only about three rounds around my apartment complex, a distance of 500 metres per round—that too with multiple stops. Each round of 500 metres used to take 9 minutes. By Week 4, I had achieved four rounds at 8 minutes a round. By Week 8, it was six rounds at 7.5 minutes a round. Finally, I pushed it to ten rounds (5 km) at 6.5 minutes a round. Jayu would walk next to me, her senses on high alert. If my foot was placed even marginally off, her ears would pick up the slight change in the sound of my footstep and her hand would shoot out to catch me. I can't imagine the kind of stress she must have been under.

But I desperately wanted to break the 6-minutes-a-round barrier and pushed myself mercilessly. I had downloaded a stopwatch app on my phone, and I kept trying to breach this target. Finally, on one glorious day, I felt my legs move like they had springs. I was flying. I did the first round in 5.47 minutes. This was the first time ever that I had broken the 6-minute barrier for a round. But I did not stop there. I clocked 5.33 minutes in the next round. I kept up this amazing speed, round after round, beating the 6-minute barrier every single time. Then in the seventh round it happened. I stubbed my toe and flew off the ground and fell. It was a full-blooded fall. It happened so fast that even Jayu's acute senses couldn't help stop the fall.

Miraculously, I was absolutely and perfectly fine. That was also a first. In the past six-odd years, I had fallen a dozen times. Each time, I had got hurt badly. This time the fall was far worse, but I was completely unhurt. I got back on my feet. I was determined to complete the ten rounds in less than sixty minutes. I practically flew in the next three rounds, and, in spite of the fall, I managed the ten rounds in 59.3 minutes.

Even though the improvements were visible and steady, I was impatient with the speed of recovery. Ashish knew a great skeleto-muscular specialist. I went to his clinic every alternate day for three months for intense physiotherapy sessions. By the end of two months, I was able to drive again.

Kavita, Elango's wife, also spent a lot of time teaching me the basics of yoga.

While my body slowly inched back to normalcy, my mind was having a total blast. The incredible mental high I first experienced on Day 10 of the treatment continued. Every day, as I worked out for close to three hours, pushing myself to the limit, the feeling of well-being kept growing.

A lot of it was also thanks to the fact that I was devoting the rest of the time to Oops.

Some authors decide on their plots and then flesh out the characters and the details. But not me. The evolved pumpkin landing from the future, trying to save humanity from a green, grunting porcine species, took me as much by surprise as it would the reader. Every character, every paragraph, every major incident sprang onto the book totally uninvited and unannounced. Each time it happened, the sheer novelty of the characters and the audacious insanity of the plot kept me rolling on the floor, laughing. There was a heady mix of endorphins, adrenalin and humour coursing through my body.

Of course, I still could not type. My fingers were healing very slowly. So I bought Dragon NaturallySpeaking from Nuance, a voice-to-text software. It was incredibly accurate, and my speed went up from one page a day to five to six pages a day. In about four months, the first draft of *Oops the Mighty Gurgle* was ready.

I learned two things...

1. The single most important requirement for success is grit, the ability to go after the goal with tenacity, without giving up and without losing heart.
2. Life can give you a bigger high than alcohol.

21. Author

Writing a book, though a commendable feat, is not enough by a long shot. You have to find a publisher brave enough to publish the damn thing.

It was in the October of 2011 that I typed 'The End' and declared my first novel complete. Even as I wiped the sweat off my brow, I had already embarked on the next step: that of finding a publisher or literary agent. Since I was absolutely convinced that my book was superior to anything ever written or anything that could possibly be written in the future, I would settle only for the best publisher. For my arrogance, I would place the blame squarely on the doorstep of my informal editors, namely, Anjali Nair, a great friend, my sister-in-law Shubha, and Elango's teenage son Vidyuth, who gave me early rave reviews.

Since the book had an international appeal, I decided to first search for a publisher in the UK or US. But a vast majority of them accepted only hard copies of the manuscript. Considering the money and effort it would take to courier envelopes containing copies of a fat manuscript to the US and UK, I decided to focus only on those few who accepted email submissions. My prime target, Christopher Little (J.K. Rowling's agent), was among them. I sent off my manuscript to him and just two publishers and waited.

In the meanwhile, I also deigned to look at Indian publishers. I did extensive web research and perfected the art of snaring a publisher. I am sharing this well-researched process with you just in case you also have ambitions in that direction.

- Go online and find out the names of the publishers of all the famous books you know.
- Ask your friends and their friends if they have any contacts in these publishing houses.
- Curse when you realize that friends do not have any big connections.
- Settle for whatever they have and get introduced to editors through aforementioned friends or friends' friends.
- Send your synopsis to all the aforementioned publishers.
- Curse your cousin BalC who worked in a company called Synopsys when you realize that you have misspelled the word 'synopsis' in all your mails.
- Wait week after week for rejections to pour in, pretending you are aiming for thirteen (J.K.R. received as many before Bloomsbury accepted *Harry Potter*).
- Write stupid blog posts about how one is about to get published.

- Get a polite rejection from Christopher Little and mutter, 'No wonder J.K.R. sacked him.'
- Get impatient and start the process of self publishing through Createspace, which asks you to cough up an enormous sum of $3,000, muttering, 'God, forgive them, for they know not what they miss.'
- Chance upon an old friend called P. Venky, who introduces you to his friend called Chanty, who introduces you to Westland, a leading publisher.
- Keep sending reminders to Westland, thanking god all the while that they have not responded, being pretty sure that any reply would be a polite rejection.
- Get a mail from a totally strange being called Sayoni Basu, who calls herself a Primary Platypus of Duckbill Publishers, saying they are an associate of Westland focused on children's and young adults' literature, and that she loves the manuscript.
- Thank god profusely for creating some sensible people like Sayoni Basu (never mind the moniker of Primary Platypus).
- Prostrate yourself and accept whatever the terms in the contract with utmost gratitude.

The book was launched in November 2012. And it was nominated in the 'Best Children's Publication' category at the Comic Con India Awards 2012.

But merely getting the book published was not enough for me. I wanted to sell 1,00,000 copies. It was, of course, a totally unrealistic dream. An Indian-authored children's book that sells 10,000 copies is considered a bestseller, since the books that sell in this category are mostly written by foreigners. I pulled out all stops, pestering all my friends until the poor souls bought their copies out of sheer fear of coming face to face with me without an *Oops* in hand.

It was worse when I travelled by plane. I would strike up a conversation with the co-passenger, and, before he knew it, convert him into an Oops follower.

I had to draw the line finally when my wife found out that I was playing online Scrabble with the sole purpose of springing the Amazon link for *Oops the Mighty Gurgle* on the unsuspecting opponents, often putting them off their bingos. She viciously told me to desist.

But I hit the jackpot when a classmate, Sharad, forwarded my mail about the book to his boss at SunGard, an American software services company. The authorities there invited me to be a speaker at their annual conference. I had never done something like this before, but I was quite excited.

I thought for some time about what kind of a speech I should make and finally decided that I should just tell my life story and share whatever I had learned. I had a rough idea about the incidents I would cover and made four slides.

The talk was pretty much like my book—totally extempore and humorous. At the end of the session, I was told by many people that it had come straight from my heart. I believe the employees voted it the best part of the evening.

SunGard was nice enough to buy copies of the book in bulk, make me autograph them and give one to each member of the audience.

Suddenly I hit upon a method to sell hundreds of copies of my book. All I had to do was persuade corporates to invite me as a speaker to their seminars and conferences.

What Sharad and Akila (the head of SunGard's operations) had given me was much more than a new avenue to sell *Oops*. They had given me an opportunity to share my experience and motivate others to whatever extent I could. They had given me a chance to touch the lives of many people in a positive manner. That gave me a high. I knew this was what I wanted to do.

I learned two things...

1. There is nothing as exhilarating as touching the lives of people positively.

2. If you are trying to persuade your co-passenger on a flight to buy your book as soon as he lands, it is best to wait till he has gone to the loo and come back. Otherwise, halfway through your sales pitch, he is likely to excuse himself with a strained smile, run off to the loo and lock himself in there till the flight lands.

Oops

In the years following the treatment in Chicago, my nerves and muscles have continued to mend. I have reduced my maniacal workouts from three hours a day to about an hour a day. I also taught myself to swim—by watching YouTube videos. Every day, I would watch these videos intently and then practise in the pool. I can now swim about 35 metres at a stretch without having to stop. Someday I hope to be able to swim the entire length of our 50-metre pool without stopping.

My weight, which had gone up to 94 kg during the worst of my steroid days, has come down to 83 kg, fluctuating between 80 and 85 kg. My fond hope is to go down to 78 kg.

Health-wise, I am now better than I have been in a long time. I can climb steps even without the support of a railing. My arms are quite strong now. I can travel on my own, do my buttons, walk on uneven ground, look up without falling and even lift a whole pitcher of beer using just my left hand. In a nutshell, I can pretty much do everything that a normal man can do.

I am still not 100 per cent okay. I cannot run; my

balance is not perfect; and I haven't regained the bounce in my step.

It is not as if everything has been perfect after the treatment. I do have my ups and downs. There are days when I feel weaker. On the day of my first annual check-up in Chicago in 2012, I tripped and fell and fractured three of my toes. In July 2014, while I was working on the final draft of this book, I had gone for a naturopathic treatment to a place called Shantivana in Dharamsthala, Karnataka, and slipped and fell at the treatment centre. I fractured my right arm in two places. But thanks to my new and improved version of Dragon, I managed to complete the work without a problem.

Even if more such issues come up in future, I will not stop trying. Every problem has a solution. I am sure I will cure myself completely sooner or later. Every once in a while I still have vivid dreams of sprinting energetically.

I had stopped working completely for a year after my treatment. Subsequently, since Jayu got transferred, we all moved to Bangalore.

Anurag Behar, the CEO of the Bangalore-based Azim Premji Foundation and a very close friend, was kind enough to put me in touch with the HR people there. Being an extraordinarily conscientious and upright gentleman, he completely kept himself out of the hiring loop. Luckily for me, they found my profile interesting enough. I now consult part-time with the foundation and contribute in whatever little way to a wonderful and world-changing initiative—that of improving the levels of education in government schools in India. Here, I met some extraordinary human beings who have dedicated their lives to improving the quality of education in the country.

I also work for an amazing start-up called Zentron Labs, founded by a close friend, Krishnan, in the space of machine vision. We help companies improve the quality of their production by enabling 100 per cent quality inspection at high speeds using computer vision and software. The solutions are useful for companies in virtually every segment: automotive, electronics, agriculture, horticulture, food etc. This can substantially improve the standing of Indian companies in the global market by ensuring far better quality offerings. I am relearning the basics of engineering and enjoying this immensely. I am also able to leverage my contacts and my business experience. I enjoy spending time with the young people in this organization.

My second book in the *Oops* series, *Oops and the Planet of the Apps*, is now with editors. It is as wacky as *Oops the Mighty Gurgle*—no mean feat. I am also currently writing a fantasy fiction trilogy for young adults.

The inspiration for writing this book came from Anna, a classmate and dear friend, who has been dogged by various disorders all her life. When I read her life story, I felt that I too have a story to tell.

I got over my 'spirituality' after I figured out that one could be higher on life than on booze.

I have two visions which constantly drive me.

First: to become the most prolific science writer for

children in the world. To achieve this end, I have now started learning science all over again. As of now, I have enrolled for eight online courses in various science streams in Coursera and Udacity—in the fields of genetics, nano-technology, quantum physics, neurology and so on.

Second: I want to touch a million lives positively—through my books, definitely, but also through my talks. As of August 2014, I have already given talks in nine corporate organizations. I have also conducted my Oops-based workshops in a dozen schools and book events. The sessions are hilarious and have the kids rolling with laughter while simultaneously giving them some interesting scientific knowledge.

I have also modified the motivational talk and delivered it to 500 high school students at The Heritage School, Gurgaon. The children were transfixed and highly inspired. I know this is my true calling. I want to talk to kids and help shape their minds and lives. I want to become a YouTuber and share funny videos for kids—videos which will nevertheless deliver strong positive messages.

I know when it comes to pushing the above agenda, I am quite persistent and possibly a pain in the neck. Many of my friends have borne the brunt of it! Forgive me, my friends, I promise to continue pushing you relentlessly to buy my books, invite me for talks, send my introduction to your children's schools, etc.

There are a few rules I have laid down for myself in life:

1. Never look at what could have been. There is nothing more wasteful or more demoralizing than brooding

on what could have been. What-could-have-beens are actually never-have-beens and almost always never-will-bes. Every day, every moment, one must accept reality as it is and plan for the future, completely cognizant and accepting of that reality. Find solutions based on today's reality and do not brood on what would never be.

2. The buck always stops with me. There is never any point blaming others for the difficulties you are in or for not being able to complete a task at work. Externalizing a problem is the act of the weak. If a colleague or a friend or a relative fails to deliver on commitments, which in turn impacts your life adversely, either convince or motivate them, do the job yourself or find someone else to do it. Whatever you do, take ownership of the deliverable instead of blaming the result on someone else or, worse, some circumstance.

3. Make every moment count. Once you have been through a situation in which you believe you will become a vegetable soon, and then you are given a new lease of life, you realize just how much you want to pack into it. Today, whatever I do, I do with 110 per cent of my being. I have only about forty more active years ahead of me at best. I have so much to accomplish. I feel terrible that each day has only twenty-four hours.

4. Be the cheerleader, always. Be the one to spread positivity. Always lift people's spirits when you enter

a room or a group. Look at the funny side of things and, when you can, make people around you laugh.

5. Do not expect life to be fair. There is no divine computer that keeps track of all the good and bad things that happen to you and ensures that the net result is just rewards for your actions. But if you grit your teeth and hang on long enough when the chips are down, life will eventually turn around and become unfair in your favour.

6. Thank god every day for all the things you have: your spouse, your children, parents, relatives, friends, your arms, your legs… There are so many wonderful things god has given us that we take for granted.

7. Return the kindness shown by all friends, relatives and others—not necessarily by being kind to them but by being kind to those in need.

8. Never keep a grudge. As a friend of mine, Michael, once said, bottling up anger and resentment is like drinking poison and expecting the other person to die. Resentment hurts only oneself. Life is way too short to waste on negative emotions.

Finally, I would like to leave you all with a poem which has touched me deeply and which I recite at every forum where I speak.

Invictus

William Ernest Henley

Out of the night that covers me,
Black as the pit from pole to pole,
I thank whatever gods may be
For my unconquerable soul.

In the fell clutch of circumstance
I have not winced nor cried aloud.
Under the bludgeonings of chance,
My head is bloody, but unbowed.

Beyond this place of wrath and tears
Looms but the horror of the shade,
And yet the menace of the years
Finds and shall find me unafraid.

It matters not how strait the gate,
How charged with punishments the scroll,
I am the master of my fate:
I am the captain of my soul.

Always remember: You are the master of your fate; you are
the captain of your soul.

Index

Acknowledgements

For helping me during the toughest period of my life, I would like to thank:

My immediate family—Jayu, Ananya and Advay—who are always there for me and who have sacrificed so much for me.

My parents and Appa, who guided me, blessed me and enriched my life.

My brother and sister-in-law, and Jayu's sister and her husband, all of whom supported us when the chips were down.

My relatives and friends who showered so much love on me—visiting me, Skyping with me, mailing me, calling me, buying my books, encouraging my talks, fixing up talks for me, taking me and my family on vacations, and reaching out to offer me jobs or financial support.

My teachers and bosses who shaped me and made me what I am today.

My colleagues and ex-colleagues, so many of whom held my hand—literally—carried my bags, fetched me coffee or food at buffets, and even tied my shoelaces when I couldn't.

My doctors and nurses, especially Dr Richard Burt, who gave me my life back.

All those hundreds of people who listened to my talks, laughed, nodded and told me they felt inspired.

All those hundreds of children who laughed delightedly and absorbed like sponges the knowledge I passed on in my wacky science talks.

I know a simple thanks will never suffice. I will not be able to repay all your kindness in my lifetime. But I promise that I will pass on that kindness whenever there is the slightest opportunity to do so. I will make sure I use this life, which all of you have helped stabilize, to spread positive energy.

A Note about RamGVallath.com

RamGVallath.com is my attempt at reaching out to millions of people. As you might have guessed, I suffer from a rather split personality and have some very diverse interests. RamGVallath.com will be an umbrella site that will bring together all of these. The various segments I am focusing on are:

1. *I Am Unchallenged:* In this space, I would like to share stories of courage and bravery of those who are undergoing physical hardships due to illnesses and disorders. The stories of how they have overcome great difficulties and spread cheer and hope around them can motivate us all. If you are one of those 'unchallenged' or know someone who is, I will be delighted to offer this platform to share that story and I will personally interview each person and write the story.

2. *Ouch to Oops score:* Visit the site and take a quick test to see where you personally stand in the 'Ouch to Oops' continuum. Are you taking on life cheerfully or are you struggling with mental demons? Do you

chill out in life or do you have a stick stuck in a strategic place? Take the test and share it with your friends (optional).

3. *Wacky science videos:* I hope I eventually get around to making these. The idea is to make science interesting by mixing it with loads of humour. This segment would be aimed at a narrow age band of 9 to 99.

So do visit www.RamGVallath.com and sign up. I promise to make it active and interesting.

You can also follow my page 'RamG Vallath' on Facebook or follow me on Twitter @ramgvallath.